A Spider Steeped

The Shakespeare Murders, Vol. 4

John Paulits

A Wings ePress, Inc.
Mystery

Wings ePress, Inc.

Edited by: Jeanne Smith
Copy Edited by: Christie Kraemer
Executive Editor: Jeanne Smith
Cover Artist: Trisha FitzGerald-Jung

All rights reserved

Wings ePress Books
www.wingsepress.com

Copyright © 2021 by: John Paulits
ISBN-13: 978-1-61309-534-8

Published In the United States Of America

Wings ePress Inc.
3000 N. Rock Road
Newton, KS 67114

Dedication

For Lizzie

***

One

Dearest Kristy,

I know you're surprised to hear from me. It's been far too long since we've seen one another. Is it really six years?! I'm married now, you know—for the past three years, actually. We'll talk about that when I see you.

I know all about you. I came across the Downtown Express newspaper article about you and your acting group—AWB Theatre Company! I'm impressed!!! I've wondered many times whether you kept up your acting, and I see you have—big time!! As you know, I gave up any chance I had to act because of all the other things I had to deal with back then, but I'm reasonably settled now. I miss our acting together, hanging out together, rooming together...It was such fun—while it lasted. Did anything ever end with such a crash? Well, never mind about that.

Remember the day we met the two sailors? That made freshman year at good old Boston U.; don't you think?

Anyway, having found you at the Bouwerie Lane Theatre, I don't want to lose you again. I'm writing to invite you for a visit. I'm only ninety minutes away from New York City, and only thirty minutes from your hometown of beautiful Brunton, PA. You must get some time off—between plays, maybe? I got the impression from the article that you and this Mark Louis are an item. Please bring him along. I'd love to meet him. But don't worry, our secrets will remain our secrets! And you must meet Raven, my darling little girl. You were there when her story began. Trust me, the story has improved since then. I've included a photo of Raven, Pete, and me. My phone number is on the back. Call and let's set up a visit. I miss you. I haven't had a friend like you since...since I had a friend like you!

Love,

Erin

Mark Louis read the letter and tossed it onto the pile of papers cluttering the end of the long, wooden picnic-style dining table.

"You've never mentioned much about college, and I can see why. The day you met the two sailors? Really?"

Kristy King smiled and batted her eyelids innocently.

"I want to know what happened when you met the two sailors."

Kristy picked up the letter and pointed to another line. "Read this part."

Mark read aloud, "Our secrets will remain our secrets."

"We complimented them on their uniforms, and they took us to lunch."

"Did they keep their uniforms on the whole time?"

Kristy smiled coyly. "On the floor, you mean?"

"Yeah, right. So tell me again...who's this girl?"

"I never mentioned her because it's too awful a memory to dredge up. Her story's right up your alley, though."

"So join me in my alley and regale me." Mark took Kristy by the hand and led her into the bedroom of their new apartment.

They'd moved out of Mark's shabby, one-room apartment on Avenue B, glad to leave it to the roaches. Mark had only recently learned that Kristy came from a wealthy family, a fact she'd kept from him as long as possible. With her background out in the open, Kristy insisted she had no reason not to spend some of her money on the two of them, so she rented a spacious loft on Greene Street in Soho, which they now called home.

They undressed quickly and fell into bed, Kristy's long, black hair fanning out across the pillow.

"Erin was my college roommate for a year. It all changed after the killing." She studied Mark, her eyebrows raised, and she waited for his reaction.

"The killing?" Mark pulled himself into a sitting position. "You mean a murder?"

"Got your attention, have I?"

"Yes, you do. Let's hear. You are a woman full of surprises."

Kristy nestled her head onto Mark's shoulder and told him the story.

"Erin was pretty much all alone in the world. Her parents were gone, and the aunt she lived with during high school was as happy to see Erin leave for college as Erin was to go. After freshman year, she and I moved out of the dorm and into an apartment. We both stayed in Boston for the summer, and she met Jeremy Casterbridge, a School of Communications student like us. She liked meeting new guys."

Mark frowned. "I remember the sailors."

"Stop. She seemed really taken by Jeremy, and by September, he'd gotten her pregnant."

"Jesus!"

"In October, we were all doing Shakespeare together—*The Winter's Tale*. She played Hermione, the aggrieved and wrongly accused wife, Jeremy played Leontes, the jealous husband, and I played Paulina, unfailing friend to Hermione."

"You did this play at the school?"

"Yep. Our first organized stab at Shakespeare. It's a tough play, but we were pretty good, as I recall. Anyway, I forget who started out as Polixenes, the king Leontes accuses Hermione of fooling around with, but he got mono and dropped out, and a fellow named Lenny York, a theatre major, stepped in. Guess what?"

"My guess is Hermione *was* fooling around with Polixenes."

"Certainly flirting around. Erin never told me how intense the fooling around got."

"And this is while she was pregnant?"

"Yes."

"Did she make a decision about the baby? About this Jeremy?"

"Don't rush me. So Jeremy learns that Erin's been out for coffee a couple times with this guy Lenny, and believe me, he didn't like it. I heard one argument he and Erin had in our apartment. Jeremy told her—ordered her—to stop seeing Lenny. If they were going to have the baby, he said she couldn't be seeing other men.

"Erin screamed at him that she didn't know whether she wanted the baby or not, and Jeremy exploded. He called her names to make you cringe. Seems he had come from a very strict Catholic background. His family wanted him to go to Boston College, but he rebelled and chose BU."

"His background didn't keep him from conceiving a child out of wedlock."

"Out of wedlock," Kristy chuckled. "You can be so quaint. Anyway, on and on Jeremy ranted about Erin quitting school and going to live with his parents, who would support them both—he came from money—while he finished his last year of school. Well, Erin wouldn't consent to that in a million years. After more name-calling and screaming, Jeremy stormed out."

"All this time the play's going on?"

"It ran for three weekends in October, and this big fight happened on the final weekend of the play. To celebrate the close of the play, the cast went out to a restaurant a few blocks from campus, I forget the name of the place."

"Bohemia?"

"Oh, nicely played, but no. Anyway, Jeremy and Lenny were old enough to drink, and so they did. Bad idea. As the party wound down, Lenny and Jeremy got into it over Erin. Jeremy told Lenny, in front of everybody, to stay away from his wife."

"His wife?"

Kristy shrugged. "His word. Lenny scoffed, and said Erin wasn't anybody's wife. Jeremy let loose with, 'She's having my baby. That's makes her my wife.' Lenny looked like he'd been shot, and before anybody could intervene, Jeremy and Lenny were pushing and punching."

Kristy stopped.

"Go on," Mark urged.

"People separated them, and we all left, but according to two witnesses, Jeremy waited for Lenny outside of Lenny's apartment building. The confrontation ended up with Jeremy punching Lenny, who fell backwards and struck his head on a cement block bordering the entrance to the building. He didn't get up and died the next day in the hospital."

"Holy shit."

"To make a long story short, Jeremy went to jail for manslaughter, and Erin dropped out of school the next week and went back to her aunt. She and I exchanged a few emails, and I called a few times, but things moved on, and I stopped trying to track her down."

"And Jeremy?"

"I have no idea. This letter she sent to the theatre is the first I've heard from her in nearly six years. Some story, eh?"

"The child she mentions in the letter, Raven, she's the child?"

"Must be if she says I was there for the beginning of the story. She'd be five, I guess, by now."

"Pete is her husband?"

"You read what I read. Pete's a stranger to me."

"Well? You want to go visit her?"

"I do, but I want you to come, too."

"I wouldn't miss it. Erin sounds like a fascinating woman. What article was she talking about?"

Kristy shrugged. "It must have been the *Downtown Express* article that came out during our run of *Twelfth Night*."

"Way back in February?"

"Must be. There haven't been any others."

"Now, about those sailors."

"Who?"

"The sailors. The sailors. You remember. Popeye and Bluto. I want to know about those sailors."

"It's a secret, matey," Kristy growled and launched herself at Mark.

Mark laughed and fought back. Before very long, though, their fighting dissolved into a peace conference of staggering proportions.

Two

AWB's summer presentation of *Richard III* had closed after a two-week extension, and rehearsals for *Lady Windermere's Fan*, due to open in two weeks, proceeded so smoothly that Mark decided to close the theatre for one week and give everyone some time off. They would take up rehearsals the following Sunday and open the next to last Thursday in October. *Richard III* had played to ninety-seven percent capacity, the actors felt good about themselves, and the company happily accepted the week off.

Bright and early on an October Wednesday, Kristy and Mark set out for Pleasantville, Pennsylvania, and a two-night visit with Erin Blakely followed by a visit to Kristy's mother.

"Excited?" Mark asked as he negotiated the entrance ramp to the New Jersey Turnpike in their rented Impala.

"More nervous than excited."

"Why nervous?"

"Something about the way Erin sounded on the phone. Like my coming was an accomplishment of hers. I sensed some weird satisfaction in her voice."

"I'm not quite following you."

"I'm not quite following myself. Oh, well. It's only until Friday morning. Looking forward to seeing my mother?"

Mark was not looking forward to seeing Kristy's mother, Betty, again, but he nodded abstractedly, feigning concentration on the road. He and Betty shared a secret each vowed to the other to take to the grave. Mark slid a Vivaldi CD into the car's sound system and suggested Kristie lie back and relax. Anything to forestall having to talk to her about her mother.

Pleasantville was a small town of some 2,500 people nestled in the countryside of Pennsylvania. Erin lived in a large house on the edge of town, and when Mark pulled into the driveway, a young woman charged out the front door toward them.

Kristy laughed and called, "Erin," as she and Mark left the car.

The two women embraced, and Kristy introduced Mark. Erin threw her arms around Mark's shoulders and planted a strong kiss on his lips.

"Any boyfriend of Kristy's is a boyfriend of mine." She laughed and said, "Remember our motto?"

Kristy waggled her finger at her. "Erin, you promised our secrets would be our secrets."

Erin laughed. "Whoops. Wait. Wait, I practiced. Welcome to Pleasantville...

...wherein our entertainment shall shame us we will be justified in our loves...We will give you sleepy drinks, that your senses, unintelligent of our insufficience, may though they cannot praise us, as little accuse us.'"

Kristy laughed. "Act one, scene one, *The Winter's Tale.*"

"Right! Come in. Come in," Erin bubbled, taking both Kristy and Mark by the arms and leading them up the driveway and into the house.

Mark had not been prepared for a woman as beautiful as Erin. Although there was a fall chill in the air, Erin dressed in a tight, low-cut, red pullover, a very short black skirt, and red high heels. Her hug and kiss shot a bolt of uncomfortable pleasure through Mark. Erin had her brown hair pulled into a tight ponytail, and her dark, inviting eyes seasoned her warm smile with an enticing spice.

"Sit down and relax." Erin indicated a well-appointed living room, and Mark and Kristy took seats on a green sofa. "Can I get you something? A drink? A snack?"

"I could use some juice, or a soda," Mark responded.

"Me, too."

"Coming up." Erin left the living room.

"Effervescent, isn't she," Mark whispered.

"Very, and as usual. Look at this place. She's done well for herself."

Erin returned with two Diet Cokes. "Now, tell me everything. Pete's at work, and I don't pick up Raven until three-thirty, so we have plenty of time to catch up. You don't have to sit through this girl talk, Mark."

"I want to hear about the two sailors from freshman year."

Erin's eyes widened. "He read my letter?"

"I let him," Kristy replied with a glance at Mark.

"Well," Erin began, "I'll answer you of your lady's tricks and mine, when we were girls; pretty girls we were then, too."

"Isn't that...?" Kristy struggled to remember.

Erin laughed. "A very bastardized line from the play. One of my lines. Mark, we were at our best in the adventure with the sailors. Classic!"

"No 'our' or 'we.' All your doing. I forego any credit."

"This is a terrible way to start reminiscing—telling tales on ourselves."

Mark frowned. "Are you certain I should really hear this? Am I certain I really want to hear this?"

"Relax and drink your soda," Erin said with a smile. "You might as well know the worst right off. Kristy and I were walking along the Charles River behind the school on a beautiful day, and these two young and gorgeous sailors began to chat us up, remember?"

"I do."

"We decided to have some fun with them."

Mark interrupted. "Uh, maybe I better—"

"Shhh!" Erin ordered. "Kristy and I always complained to one another about the food in the dorm—Café 700 we called it after the address of the dorm—700 Commonwealth Avenue. These two young men invited us to have lunch—go for coffee and something to eat. I demurely told them no, of course, but they kept at us. Typical government-issue Lotharios. Finally, I got so annoyed, I told them Kristy and I were roommates and had recently gotten over the flu and couldn't eat much, but we might go for some soup at Mango. Remember the Thai restaurant on Commonwealth?"

Kristy rolled her eyes. "I do."

"They gave each other a look like whoa! Soup! Cheap dates. When we sat down, I ordered lobster for Kristy and me, and a nice range of appetizers and side dishes. I told them we felt much better since we'd met them." Erin laughed. "You should have seen their faces. Instead of three-dollar soup, we dined on twenty-one-dollar lobsters each plus a lot of other."

"They ordered soup," said Kristy.

"They did! I remember. I thanked them so much for our nearly hundred dollar lunch—they could barely scrape together enough money to pay the bill." Erin laughed again. "I told them I knew an elegant restaurant downtown where we could go later for dinner, but they said they needed to be back on their ship."

Kristy smiled and shook her head.

"No wonder recruitment in the Navy's been down," said Mark.

"We were dorm heroes for a week after we told the story around."

Kristy demurred. "You told the story around. You. I claim no credit. I went along for the ride. An innocent observer."

"An innocent partaker. Even though all of our stories are equally innocent, Mark, you really shouldn't hear any more of them. Some of them might be...misinterpreted." Erin laughed again.

"You may be right. I'll get our things from the car and put them...?"

"Top of the stairs to the left. You'll find a bottle of wine lying on the bed."

"Wine. I'm impressed," said Mark, giving Erin an appreciative glance, and he left to get their bags.

~ * ~

After a casual lunch in Erin's bright, spacious and marble counter-topped kitchen, all three drove into town in Erin's Lexus to pick up Raven.

"There's her school." Erin pulled her car up to the curb across the street from a one-story building with children's drawings looking out from a number of classroom windows. "Can you wait here a sec? I need to do one chore. I won't be long."

Kristy and Mark watched her scurry into a four-story building a few storefronts down.

"Was she like this in college?" Mark asked, leaning back against Erin's car. "I'm getting worn out watching her. And did she always dress like that? You look very nice in your bulky unisex sweater, by the way."

"Don't be cute. Yes, she's always had more energy—and more men—than she knew what to do with."

"What'd you two talk about before lunch when I took a walk?"

"I told her about the theatre and about you. She feigned jealousy at my catching a six-foot-tall, blond actor. She seems to be very taken with you."

A passerby, a young man dressed in jeans and a tan sweater, bent down without pausing and looked inside Erin's car. Mark's eyes followed him down the sidewalk.

"What are you staring at?" Kristy asked.

"Some fellow gave us the once over."

"Us or me?" Kristy watched the man continue down the sidewalk and enter the same building Erin had entered. "Him?"

"Yeah."

"Who was it?"

"How do I know? I didn't get a good look at him. Your bulky sweater must have mesmerized him."

"I'll mesmerize you, buster, you mention my sweater again."

"You were telling me how taken Erin is with me, I think. Carry on."

"If I said taken, I meant impressed. Just make sure *you* don't carry on. I think you've heard enough already."

"You said your friend was a good actress?"

"Very good. Oh, here she comes."

"I'm back. Come on. I'm dying for you to meet Raven."

Older children began to stream from the school, shouting and chasing one another. Erin led her guests around to the back of the school where the smaller children waited in line in the schoolyard to be picked up, with their teachers watching over them.

"Mommy!" cried a young girl, who tapped her teacher and pointed. The teacher nodded, and the little girl ran toward Erin.

Erin lifted the child into her arms. "Raven, these are mommy's friends. This is Mark, and this is Kristy. Mommy went to school with Kristy."

"Kindergarten?"

Erin laughed. "No, college. Isn't she beautiful?"

"I see why you call her Raven," Kristy said, smiling. "I've never seen such gorgeous hair." Thick waves of black hair reached to the child's shoulders and cupped her head like an elegant waterfall. "It's as dark as mine." Kristy had glittering black hair, a token of her one-quarter Asian heritage.

"How did you know to call her Raven?" Mark asked. "Wasn't she a bald-headed baby?"

Erin laughed. "Not entirely bald. I always liked the name, and by a stroke of fate, it fit."

"I'm hungry," Raven whined.

"We always have a snack after school," Erin explained as she stroked the child's cheek. "Let's go home for cookies, and Raven will tell us about her day."

Erin put the child down, took her by the hand, and led the way back to the car.

Three

Kristy laughed when she looked inside the pots on top of the stove. "Tell me you're not making our old standby." Mark and Pete chatted in the living room.

"What else? And it's become a favorite of Raven's. I knew it would bring back memories for you."

"Spaghetti, Mommy?"

"Mommy and Kristy used to cook lots of spaghetti when we lived together."

"We must have eaten spaghetti I don't know how many times those few months in the apartment. Was there anything we didn't put into it at different times? We sank to our lowest, I think, when we cut up hot dogs and topped the spaghetti with *Cheez Whiz*."

"I think you had too much cocktail hour when you cooked that night."

"What was I thinking? I get goose bumps thinking about it now."

"Can we have it next time, Mommy? The whiz thing?"

"Maybe when it's just me and you, sweetie. I don't think Daddy would go for it. Go play a while. I'll call you for dinner."

Kristy helped Raven down from the stool where she perched, and the child wandered off.

"So, tell me about Pete," Kristy said while Erin rolled some ground beef into tiny balls. "I never thought I'd see you settled down with a car salesman. They certainly weren't your type at BU."

Erin frowned. "He's not a car salesman. He owns the dealership. Does this house look like it belongs to a car salesman? The car salesmen work for him. As to why? I needed...you know. It was a drag being on my own—a single mom, no family except a crotchety old aunt who barely tolerated me. I struggled, believe me. Pete came along and treated me very well. He seemed to like Raven a lot." She paused.

By the way Erin accented "seemed," Kristy sensed an uncomfortable relationship had formed between Raven and Pete.

Erin paused, and for the lack of anything better to say, Kristy offered to help prepare the dinner. "Can I do anything? Boil some water?"

Erin shook her head. "Things have changed in the three years we've been together. We got married only two months after we met. You know how men are. Once they have what they want...and you know how I am," she added softly with a brief smile. "It's always better to have a man chasing you than to let him catch you. You and Mark ever talk about getting married?"

"Never comes up."

For a moment, Erin forgot the ground beef sizzling in a frying pan and said, "Don't let it. I miss back then when everything was for play. Now...it's all so real. Being married is very real. I hoped Pete was for real. Raven is wonderfully real. I'm not complaining; don't get me wrong." She gave a soft laugh. "But I'm glad claustrophobia isn't fatal."

"Erin Blakely, are you trying to tell me something?"

Erin put on a thoughtful look, one an actress might use. "Maybe later. I have some cooking to do now. Go see how the boys are. Open up some wine for them."

Kristy took a bottle of Kendall Jackson Chardonnay from the refrigerator and uncorked it.

"You'll find glasses at the bar in the living room. Dinner in about forty-five minutes."

When Kristy entered the living room, she heard Pete telling Mark how he'd met Erin.

"From standing next to one another in a car wash to the altar in two months. Life takes some strange turns. Erin told me you and Kristy met working in the theatre."

"We were in different plays but hung out at the same place, a bar named Phebe's."

"Ah, the stash has been cracked open," Pete said with a smile when Kristy entered the room. "Let me get glasses and a bucket of ice."

Raven popped quickly into the room. "Oh, I thought I heard Mommy." She spun away and exited.

Pete, a slim man whose sandy hair had already begun to thin, stood three inches shorter than Mark's six feet and looked a good ten years older than his wife.

Kristy put the bottle on the coffee table and sat next to Mark on the sofa.

"Dinner in less than an hour," Kristy announced.

"You okay?" Mark whispered while Pete grabbed some glasses from the bar. "You have a funny look."

"I'm okay."

Pete returned and distributed the wine.

"So, what was Erin like in college?" Pete asked as he poured. "The same shy, retiring type she is now?" He rattled the wine bottle into the ice bucket.

"Erin is Erin," Kristy said, smiling. "Things never bogged down when she was involved. We were assigned the same dorm room freshman year in Warren Towers and took an apartment together in the summer. We had a blast in Boston. When the new semester started, we acted in *The Winter's Tale* and were accounted fabulous." She halted the story there. "Fun time while it lasted."

"You two must be filled with college secrets." Pete sat on a chair and leaned forward. "She doesn't tell me much about her past—although, of course, I know about the unpleasantness surrounding her leaving college, the bare bones of it, anyway. Erin says you two haven't had much contact with one another since then."

"Practically none." Kristy sipped her wine. "We kept in touch briefly, but..."

The phone rang, and Pete rose to get it.

"You look funny," Mark whispered insistently. "Don't tell me you don't. What's up?"

Kristy seesawed her hand. "Something is rotten in the state of Pennsylvania."

"I know that line's not from *Winter's Tale*."

"I'll talk to you later."

"Yes, Erin's here," they heard Pete say. "Who shall I say is calling... Hello? Hello?" Pete replaced the phone. "He hung up on me."

Kristy smiled. "Maybe a shy telemarketer."

"Ha! Never met one of those. Ah, here she is." Pete stood as Erin entered the living room.

"Water's boiling. Meatballs are in the sauce. I thought I'd sneak in and have a quick sip of wine."

Pete poured another glass of wine. "Here you go, honey."

"Thanks." Erin sat next to Kristy.

"Hi, Mommy." Raven rushed into the room.

"Careful, Raven." Erin lifted her glass high. "Don't bump Mommy's arm."

Raven snuggled next to her mother on the sofa.

Pete said, "Raven, there's no room for you there. Get yourself another chair."

"She's fine, Pete."

Pete did not react.

"How do you like your school?" Kristy asked, leaning forward to address Raven.

Raven gave a peek at Pete as if wondering whether she should participate or not.

"Kristy asked you a question, Raven," Pete said in an even tone.

"It's good."

"She'll talk more when she gets to know you better," Erin interrupted. She spoke in the same even tone as Pete.

The doorbell rang.

"Who can that be?" Erin said. "Pete."

Pete put his glass on the coffee table and answered the door. The others listened.

"Yes, she's home," came Pete's voice. "Erin..." Pete came back into the living room followed by a man in his late twenties, with dark hair, dressed casually in jeans and a denim jacket.

"Mommy, you spilled!" exclaimed Raven.

Erin's wine glass broke apart on the floor, and the wine spread slowly over the polished wood. Pete moved to blot it up with a handful of napkins.

Kristy gasped and grabbed Mark's hand.

Erin rose. "Oh, my God! Jeremy."

"Hand me some more napkins, Raven." Pete pointed to the stack of napkins.

Jeremy's eyes shifted from Erin to the shattered wine glass to the little girl handing over a wad of napkins to her stepfather. "Hello, Raven. I'm glad to finally get a chance to meet you."

Raven stepped behind her mother.

"Erin, who is this?" Pete asked, rising from the floor. "Who are you?"

Pete gulped the rest of his wine and slid the damp napkins into his empty glass.

"My name is Jeremy Casterbridge, and I happen to be—"

"Jeremy, what are you doing here?" Erin burst out.

"Do you mean why am I not still..." He glanced at Raven. "...incarcerated? My time is up, and I'm a free man now. You and I have a great deal to discuss."

"Erin, who is this man?" Pete insisted.

"My God," Erin mumbled. "Raven, will you go up to your room

while Mommy talks to our new visitor? Only for a little while, honey. Pete, take her up."

"No," Raven snapped, throwing a tense look Pete's way. "I'll go myself."

The adults watched the child run through the living room, her dark hair bouncing. She peeked over her shoulder to make sure she wasn't being followed, and reaching one hand up to the banister, she climbed the stairs.

"Shall we all sit?" Jeremy suggested. He helped himself to a chair and pulled it nearer the sofa. "To answer your question: surely Erin must have mentioned me to you. Jeremy Casterbridge. College boyfriend. Guilty of manslaughter. Father of your beautiful little stepdaughter."

Pete threw Erin a quick, cold glance, and then glared at their visitor. "You have a lot of nerve waltzing in here like this. Did you call and hang up earlier?"

Jeremy ignored Pete's question. "Child doesn't seem to take much to you."

"Jeremy," Erin interrupted, "why are you here?"

Jeremy surveyed the wine glasses. "Everyone's drinking wine but me."

"Just say your piece," Pete snapped.

"My piece? Okay. I'm here, Erin, to let you know I'm around, and I expect to see my daughter whenever I want to."

"Jeremy, you know it's not that simple," said Erin. "You can't expect to just appear in Raven's life and confuse her. I'll not allow it. Where are you living?"

"I've been out a month, and I've been home. My parents, at least, did not desert me. They've forgiven me and urged me to do the right thing. Would have been nice if they'd told me what the right thing was. One right thing, though, is to make up to Raven for the lack of a father."

"I've been a father to Raven for the past three years," Pete said, giving Jeremy a hard stare.

"Not from what I saw a few minutes ago."

"Look, pal, I know I speak for Erin and me both when I say you're not welcome here. You'll have to go. Now."

Jeremy ignored Pete. "Erin, pick a time and a place where we can sit down alone and discuss my being a part of Raven's life. I'm looking to get a job around here. My parents will help me out until I've got myself back together. They would have taken care of you, too, if you'd let them, but I see you've managed to struggle through." He gazed pointedly around the living room. "Not a surprise."

"Do I have to call the police?" Pete threatened. "Someone with your history surely wouldn't want to be reported to the police."

"My history happens to be the result of an accident, pure and simple. A bad accident, but an accident nonetheless." Jeremy rose, challenging Pete.

"Wait, wait," Mark interjected. "Sit down. Sit down. This is no good."

"And you are?" Jeremy asked.

"A friend, visiting. What you're asking for is probably going to need lawyers and court orders. You can't do what you're asking with such informality."

"I can if Erin agrees to it. I don't care how, but I want it done, and the first step, Erin, is for us to meet and talk." Jeremy sat down.

"My wife is not meeting you. She's not talking to you," Pete said, emboldened by Jeremy's retreat. "I warn you...I'm letting the police know about your visit here and your threats."

"Threats. What threats?" Jeremy scoffed. "I'm not surprised you feel threatened, but I've made no threats."

"Pete, let me handle this," said Erin softly.

"There's nothing to handle," Pete answered.

"Pete." Erin addressed her husband. "I said I'd handle it."

Jeremy gave a snorting chuckle. "That's the Erin I knew, going her own way no matter what anyone says to the contrary."

Pete crossed his arms, seething.

"Do you have a phone number?" Erin asked Jeremy.

"Cell phone, courtesy of Mom and Dad." He pulled out a business card he'd picked up somewhere, took a pen from his jacket pocket, and jotted the phone number on the back of the card. He passed it to Erin, who glanced at it. The Happy Wok Restaurant, it read.

"I'll call you," she promised.

"Tomorrow. I'm in a dinky apartment on the edge of Main Street, and I'm available twenty-four seven. Nice meeting all of you." He rose. "I'll see myself out."

Everyone watched Jeremy make his way to the door.

When they heard the door close, Erin said, "Well, that was unexpected, to say the least."

"You're not meeting him," Pete burst out hotly. "The nerve to simply sashay in here and give orders."

"What do you think, Kristy?" asked Erin.

Mark answered before Kristy could. "Look, this has to be kept among the three of you. This Jeremy character probably has some legal rights in this. I wouldn't really know, though."

"A felon?" Pete snapped. "Why should a convicted felon have any rights about anything?"

"I don't know that he does," said Mark, keeping his tone level. "But he might. Do you have a lawyer? Talking to him or her would be your best move, I think. Talk to your lawyer."

"I'll talk to him," Pete growled. "I'll get a restraining order, and he won't be allowed within a mile of us."

Erin breathed a deep sigh. "I don't know what this's done for everyone's appetite, but let's go and rescue my meatballs. Ten minutes and dinner."

"Did the man go?" came Raven's voice from the middle of the stairs.

Erin smiled at the child. "Yes, he did, honey. Come help me. You and I'll finish making dinner." Raven completed her descent and ran to Erin, took her hand, and accompanied her into the kitchen.

"I need some air," said Pete, avoiding Mark and Kristy's gaze. "Excuse me." He stood, crossed the dining room, then passed through a pair of sliding doors into the yard.

"Boy," said Mark. "You really know how to entertain a guy."

"I told you I felt something out of whack."

"You knew this Jeremy was around?"

"No, no. I knew from the way Erin acted. It couldn't have been Jeremy, though. She clearly didn't know he was around either."

"You think we should abort our visit? These people are going to have a lot on their plate."

Kristy considered. "I'll talk to Erin. She started to tell me something in the kitchen but turned it into 'we'll talk later.' Now this. I think she wants...needs someone to talk to."

"She has Pete."

Kristy made a dismissive motion with her hand. "I think he's what she wants to talk to me about. It seems there's a snake here in Eden. She mentioned Pete and Raven don't seem to get along."

"Even her visitor picked up on that," said Mark. "The kid popped in here once before you joined us, and then again when you brought the wine. She popped right out again. She wanted mommy, and mommy only."

Kristy's eyes lit. "Mark, could Jeremy be the man you saw across from school today when we waited for Erin?"

"The guy who looked into the car?"

"Yes."

Mark shook his head. "No, I don't think so."

Erin stepped out of the kitchen. "We can finally eat."

"Let me come help," said Kristy.

"You're not leaving me alone," said Mark, glancing at the sliding doors, and he followed Kristy into the kitchen to help Erin serve the dinner.

Four

After a dreary dinner and an early night, Mark and Kristy awoke next morning to an empty house. A note from Erin invited them to help themselves to the coffee and Danish and to meet her at The Hitching Post on Main Street at 12:30 for lunch.

"I'm glad no one's here," Mark said as he poured two cups of coffee. "Pleasantville isn't living up to its name."

"What were you reading?"

"When you woke up?"

"Yes."

"I found a copy of *The Winter's Tale* on top of the dresser. Must have been Erin's acting copy. There are acting notes in the margins."

"Did you decide what we're doing after *Lady Windermere*?"

"Not yet. Thank goodness Gehring freed up some money for us from Ashley's will. We'll be able to go on like we have been for a while longer."

Gehring was the lawyer who handled legal matters for Ashley Warrington Brunner, the eponymous founder of the AWB Theatre Company. Her unexpected demise had left the theatre in financial peril, but the litigation over the will eventually freed up considerable money for the theatre company—one of the few Off-Broadway theatres to pay their permanent actors a living wage.

"We'll pick a play soon. I'm more interested in figuring out how to gracefully get us out of a very unpleasant Pleasantville."

"How could I know we'd walk into this wasp's nest?"

"No, no. I'm not blaming you. Let's make nice today and leave first thing tomorrow morning as planned. That shouldn't occasion any awkwardness."

"Deal. So how shall we kill the two hours until lunch?"

"How about a tour of Main Street? It seemed pleasant enough—no pun intended. It's our ultimate destination anyway."

"Sounds good."

~ * ~

Main Street ran for a total of five long blocks. Raven's school anchored one end of the street across from the The Hitching Post, so Mark and Kristy decided to start at the far end of the street and work their way along. They parked the car and set out.

"A bit desolate at this end," Mark commented, gazing at the dreary buildings. Municipal offices took up one side of the street and a few residences the other. Mark took a detour to inspect the holdings of the village library, one of the services housed in the municipal complex.

"They have some Shakespeare and Shaw, but not much else interesting," he reported to Kristy. "Let's try the Art Collective." They proceeded to a large room down the hallway from the library.

After twenty minutes examining some paintings, duck decoys, and a number of quilts, they stepped outside. Kristy set off toward the next block, but Mark stopped her.

"The visitor last night, Jeremy, said he lived in a small apartment at the edge of town. You think it might be over there?" Mark pointed to a rectangular two-story building with the look of an old motel. Mark led Kristy across the street. Twelve mailboxes, each labelled with a name, lined the curb along a narrow stretch of grass. They found Jeremy Casterbridge's name printed under the words 'Apartment 3.'

"Mark, let's go. I don't want to bump into him."

"Lead on."

The next three blocks held various professional offices, two antique stores, a craft shop, a bookstore, a hardware store, a clothing store, a drug store and two small restaurants. Browsing the stores painlessly filled up the time until lunch. Mark and Kristy started onto the final block at 12:30.

Kristy gestured. "Let's cross. Nothing over here but the school."

"Wait," Mark grabbed her arm. "Look there. In the same building she visited yesterday. Come. Over here."

"Behind a tree? Really?"

"Shh. Just watch."

Erin stood in the doorway facing away from them, apparently talking to someone inside the building. Mark caught a glimpse of a bare arm. The amount of hair on the arm indicated it belonged to a man.

Erin checked in both directions before stepping inside the building out of sight for a few seconds. When she reappeared, she strode pertly toward The Hitching Post. The door of the building closed on its own.

Kristy touched Mark's arm, unsettled by what she'd seen. "What do you make of that?" she asked.

"Did you see the arm? She said good-bye to a man. Why'd she step back inside at the last moment, you think?"

"I don't know."

"I hope she doesn't get around to pouring her heart out to you. I'm not eager to get any more involved in this domestic drama than we already are. I repeat. Let's conclude our visit and get out of here tomorrow morning. Come on. Lunchtime."

They crossed the street and found Erin in a booth awaiting them.

"You're right on time," Erin said, offering a wide smile. She was dressed in a tight white pullover and quite obviously had decided a bra would be too much to bear on such a beautiful day as this.

Mark struggled to keep his eyes on Erin's eyes, and said, "Lovely Main Street you have here. Good bookshop two blocks down."

"How's the day going? Get all your chores done?" Kristy asked.

Erin's smile faded. "Let's order first."

After they placed their orders, Erin said, "I dropped Raven at school, and I've been doing stuff ever since. I tried to get in to see Charlie Hegh—he's our lawyer—but he's involved in a case in Ardmore, a good hour away. I left him a message to call me. Sometime today, I have to give Jeremy a call, but I want to talk with Charlie first. I don't want him coming around the house again. Pete was beside himself last night after we went to bed. I'd never seen him so...so wild-eyed. I hope he didn't keep you awake with his ranting."

Mark shook his head slightly. "We didn't hear anything."

"Phew. Good."

"So, have you decided what to do about Jeremy?" Kristy asked.

The waiter came and placed their sandwiches and soft drinks on the table.

Erin shrugged glumly. "What do you think I should do about him?"

Kristy studied Erin's face. "You had something to tell me last night in the kitchen."

Mark grimaced inwardly, knowing Kristy was inviting trouble.

Erin shook her head slowly. "No, just the claustrophobia I mentioned. Now this. Why does everything have to be so difficult, so complicated?"

"I thought you were going to tell me you had a sweetie," Kristy whispered, in a cavalier tone of voice. "All for one but two is better. Another of our mottoes," Kristy explained to Mark, who offered her an eye roll in return.

"Believe me, I've thought about it, but it's a small town. Everybody's watching; everybody knows everybody else. There are very few secrets." Erin finally mirrored Kristy's conspiratorial smile and whispered, "Plus, the possibles are few and far between." The two women joined in fleeting laughter. "Listen to me. I'm talking like we're still playing around back in Boston." Erin's brief smiled faded. "It's more complicated than you know." She rose. "I'll be right back. Gotta pee. Nerves."

"Why are you forcing her to tell you something she otherwise wouldn't?" Mark complained. "Don't get us any deeper into this, please. Wasp's nest, remember?"

"You're the one who's always so nosy. Don't you want to know what's going on?"

"No, I don't."

Erin reappeared, and for a moment, everyone sat in silence.

Finally, Erin said, "I have to tell somebody, Kristy, and you mustn't repeat this to a soul." Erin moved her eyes to Mark.

"I'll take a walk."

"No," Kristy insisted quickly.

Mark felt Kristy's knee whack his under the table. He wondered why he hadn't done that to her earlier.

"Anything you tell me I'd tell him anyway," Kristy said, putting her hand atop Mark's for a moment.

"You two are very lucky," Erin muttered softly, and silence descended on the table again.

Mark cleared his throat and tried to redirect the conversation before Erin started in on her explanation of complicated things. "So, are you going to leave the problem of Jeremy in the hands of your lawyer? I think you should."

"I know. I know. Last night I made Pete promise not to talk to Charlie. I said I would. He was all for rushing off to confront Jeremy again today, but he doesn't really understand how complicated it is."

"Maybe not so much," Mark put in, hopefully. "The worst that could happen is a judge will decree Jeremy gets to see Raven a specified amount of time."

"I'm not certain Jeremy has any right to see Raven at all," Erin said quietly.

"Because he was in jail?" Kristy asked.

"No." She paused. "I'm not certain he's Raven's father."

"What!" Kristy burst out. "What do you mean?"

Mark closed his eyes. Too late.

"Kristy, do you remember when our good king Polixenes came down with mono and dropped out of our play?"

"I do."

"Did you ever wonder how we found a replacement so quickly?"

"No. I supposed they posted the role somewhere and…and Lenny York showed up. My God, Lenny's hair was coal black!"

"You remember. When I learned about the opening, I told Lenny about it, and he got the part immediately. We never had to post it anywhere. I met Lenny a month before I met Jeremy. You'd gone home, I remember. When you got back, Jeremy had just entered the scene. For a while I saw them both, but then I just took to Jeremy. What Jeremy detected wasn't the beginning of a romance between Lenny and me. It was the end of one."

"So, you're telling me Lenny is Raven's father?" Kristy asked, wide-eyed.

"I'm telling you I don't know. I said it's complicated. I was making love to Lenny before I met Jeremy. Then I made love to them both for a week or two. I stopped with Lenny. I don't know. It could be either one of them." Erin rubbed her hands up and down over her face.

"This is bizarre," Mark muttered.

Erin stared at her half-eaten sandwich and softly added, "I'm not real eager to explain all of this to Pete, and eventually to Raven."

Mark directed a brief look of disgust toward Kristy. To Erin he said, "Well, it will doubtless get Jeremy out of your life if you prove he isn't the father. There are simple tests to prove lineage. What Pete would make out of it…you'd be a better judge of him than Kristy or me. He already knows Raven isn't his, so…" Mark spread his hands. "…she's got to be somebody's."

Kristy added, "Or you could go on letting people believe Jeremy is the father. No other explanations needed."

"No!" Erin snapped. "Any package that comes with a lifetime of Jeremy, I certainly reject. I detest him. My only concern is Raven."

"Raven, I think, will love you unconditionally, no matter how all of this turns out," Mark offered softly.

"She's too young to understand anything now, anyway," Kristy added. "I think you do have to find out who the father really is. Raven will ask you someday."

"I suppose she will."

"What have you told her?" Mark asked. "About her father, I mean. Does she know it's not Pete?"

"I told her that her father went away and wouldn't be back."

The table stayed quiet until Mark suggested, "You should consider having your lawyer do all the explaining to Jeremy. There seems to be a streak of meanness in him you might want to avoid."

"You're right. He won't take this news passively. He won't, believe me. Oh, my. Life can be wonderful." She shook her head and sighed. "Enough of this. I'll put it in Charlie's hands, and tell him the whole story. Things will fall out as they may. I've burdened you with my life way too much. I intended for us to relive old times and have some laughs."

"We're reliving old times all right," Kristy said with a shake of her head.

"But we're a little short of laughs?" Erin asked with an apologetic smile.

"We'll be leaving first thing tomorrow morning to go visit Kristy's mom," Mark put in, wanting to get their departure firmly established. "Anything we can do for you today, though…" Mark left the sentence hang.

Erin gave Mark a grateful smile and shook her head. "Let me call Pete and arrange dinner tonight. I won't deal with any more of this until Charlie calls me. We'll have dinner outside of town undisturbed, I trust."

Erin fished in her purse for her cell phone, opened it, and scowled.

"The battery finally died. It's been warning me, but I kept putting it off."

"Want to use mine?" Kristy offered.

"No, no. I'll call Pete from home later after we pick up Raven." Erin studied the bill a moment and put a twenty and a ten down on the table. "Where's your car?"

"The other end of town," Mark answered.

"We'll pick it up later. Let's enjoy today and try to find those missing laughs I promised you. I want to take you to a gorgeous cider mill about twenty miles from here. The scenery and the cider are both out of this world."

Erin rose and Mark and Kristy followed her toward the door. Erin took Mark's arm in both of her own and hugged it tightly to her. Again, a bolt of pleasurable discomfort roller-coastered through Mark as he felt the press of Erin's breast on his arm.

"Kristy's very lucky," she said softly. She released Mark's arm and led her friends out onto Main Street.

Five

After the trip to the cider mill, Erin dropped Mark and Kristy at their car and left to pick up Raven. She told her guests to relax at home while she took Raven to the park to play. Mark took a nap while Kristy sat in the backyard and read the first two acts of *The Winter's Tale*.

Erin dropped Raven at the babysitter's house and came home to mix margaritas for a brief cocktail hour. At five-thirty, they changed clothes for dinner.

"Phew! What did she put into my margarita?" Kristy asked. "My head is spinning."

"It was a little strong. Good thing she abbreviated happy hour to happy half-hour. One of those drinks was plenty."

"You had the other half of your happy hour at lunch," Kristy said, slipping into a skirt.

"Lunch? I didn't have anything to drink at lunch."

"I mean your elbow had a happy hour. Or at least a happy moment."

"My elbow?"

"Yes, don't act innocent. When Erin hugged you to show her gratitude for your analysis of her situation."

The drink really did have Kristy spinning. Mark chose not to answer.

Kristy smiled and pulled a yellow top over her head. "Well?"

"Well what?"

"Wasn't it a happy moment?"

"Boy, you don't miss a trick. She's your buddy. Nothing I could do about it."

"Hmmm. I think I will be glad when we're out of here tomorrow morning."

"Me, too," Mark agreed. "Can't wait for my good-bye kiss, though."

Kristy glared at him.

He laughed. "Kidding. Just kidding. Hello? Kidding. I love you with all my heart and soul, darling."

"You better."

Erin called from downstairs. "Come on, you guys. I told Pete six o'clock."

Mark checked his watch. Ten minutes to six.

"Look and tell me what she's wearing," Mark said, giving Kristy a playful push out their bedroom door.

"Boy, you're really looking for trouble, aren't you?"

"All right. All right. No more teasing. I'm sorry."

Erin waited by the front door wearing a short leather jacket. She also wore very high heels and a tight black miniskirt. Kristy gave Mark a glance, and Mark feigned indifference to the whole scene.

"I'll drive," Erin said. "Ride up front with me, Mark."

Mark held the front passenger-side door open for Kristy.

"No, Erin invited you to ride up front, Mark," she said, glowering.

He frowned Kristy's way as he opened and closed the door for her, then slid into the front seat. As they drove, he did his best not to be distracted by how far Erin's skirt traveled up her thighs.

"We're going a couple miles out of town—a place Pete and I've never tried. DaVinci's. I told Pete six-ish but he's never on time anyway.

Always some indecisive customer coming in at the last moment." Erin chattered on as Mark watched the scenery go by, but Kristy's back seat silence somehow impeded his power to concentrate. He hoped it was merely the margarita at work, since in the ten months he and Kristy'd known each other she'd never shown a speck of jealousy; nor had he given her any reason to.

At six-ten, they pulled into the parking lot of a small restaurant built of stone and surrounded by greenery.

Erin scanned the parking lot. "I don't see Pete's car. Oh, well. He'll get here when he gets here."

When they reached their table, Erin took off her jacket and hung it over the back of her chair. She wore a tight, baby blue pullover with spaghetti straps whose neckline was scooped low and wide. Mark felt yet another bolt of uncomfortable pleasure and for the first few seconds could not look away. Kristy's thumb in his back recalled him. He averted his eyes as they sat, and Erin scanned the wine list. "Is red okay for everybody? Cabernet?"

"Red's fine," Mark assured her.

"Good. Let's get some appetizers while we wait."

The hot and cold antipasto assortments disappeared amid Erin's carping about Pete's lateness.

Erin checked her watch. "It's seven o'clock already. What is wrong with him? Why are men so...?" She glanced at Mark and smiled. "Why are *some* men so unreliable?"

"Maybe you should call him," said Kristy, who sipped sparingly at her wine.

Mark took Kristy's abstemious approach to mean she knew the before-dinner margarita was having its way with her.

"I guess I should. He's spoiling the whole night." She reached into her purse. "Oh, damn. Battery. Tomorrow for sure. I'll see if I can use the restaurant's phone."

"No, no. Here, use mine," Kristy suggested as Erin rose.

"No, no. I see the restaurant phone next to the register," Erin said.

"Don't be silly." Kristy reached for Erin's arm and put the phone into her hand. Erin considered a moment, then punched in a number and waited. "He's not home. Let me try work." She took a few steps away from the table. "Not there either." As Kristy and Mark took up their conversation again, Erin moved further off.

"Where'd she go?" Mark asked a moment later.

"There."

Erin stood in the far corner of the restaurant, her back to them.

"She probably doesn't want us to hear her scolding poor Pete," Kristy said.

"Why do women need to scold us?"

"Wrong question. Why do you sometimes need to be scolded? But I don't remember scolding you much. Have I?"

Mark knew the correct answer. "No, dear." He sipped his wine and waited.

"Find him?" Kristy asked, when her friend returned.

"He's nowhere. Not at home or work. Doesn't answer his cell." She shook her head and handed the phone back to Kristy. "We might as well order. He can order when he gets here. Or starve, for all I care. I'm sure you're both famished by now." They ordered and dined and chatted until, at eight-thirty, Erin said, "I don't understand what happened to him."

"Here, call home again," Kristy said. "He must be someplace."

Erin took Kristy's phone and punched in the number. "Hello, yes. Who is this? I'm Mrs. Blakely. At a nearby restaurant." She listened and a look of panic leaped into her eyes. "Yes," she mumbled into the phone, and her hand sank to the tabletop. With a look of dazed disbelief, she lifted her eyes to Mark and Kristy.

"Erin, what is it?" Kristy asked.

"Some kind of accident. A police officer answered the phone. Pete...Pete's...I don't know. We have to go."

Mark paid the bill, and they hurried to the car. The scene at Erin's house was unsettling. Two police cars with flashing lights sat in her driveway, and the lights burned inside her house. Two uniformed police officers prowled the sides of the house, flashlights in hand, scouring the ground. They looked up when Erin's car caught them in its headlights. One of the officers approached.

"What's going on?" Erin asked in alarm.

"Who are you, ma'am?" the officer asked in a neutral voice.

"I live here."

"Come with me."

Mark and Kristy followed Erin and the officer inside the house. Another officer stood inside the front door, and two men in suits stood next to the sofa in conversation.

"Lieutenant, this woman claims to live here," the officer reported before turning around and going back outside.

"Are you Mrs. Blakely?"

"Yes."

"And these folks?"

"Friends of mine. Houseguests. We were out for dinner. What's happened?"

"I have bad news for you. There was some kind of incident. A man we've identified as Peter Blakely was found outside. I'm afraid he's dead."

"Omigod!" Erin clapped her left hand to the side of her head and bent as if struck by a sudden pain. "How? What happened?"

"Sit down, please," the lieutenant said. "My name is O'Malley. Lieutenant O'Malley."

Erin, Mark, and Kristy sat on the sofa. Kristy put her arm across Erin's shoulders.

"Either he fell and struck his head…or someone struck him with a rock. Evidence indicates there were two people outside."

"Oh, Jeremy!" Erin buried her face in her hands, sobbing.

"I'm sorry? Jeremy?" O'Malley asked.

Erin could not answer. Kristy rubbed her hand across Erin's back, sighed deeply and said, "Something happened here last night, Lieutenant."

"Go on."

"A friend, former friend, of Erin's showed up unexpectedly and had an unpleasant exchange with Erin's husband." Kristy narrated enough of Jeremy and Erin's history to give the lieutenant an idea of the previous evening.

Erin spoke up. "He's done this before. To Lenny. To Lenny."

The lieutenant looked at Kristy, and Kristy related that part of Erin's history.

"I see. Any idea where we can find this Jeremy?"

Erin quickly shook her head. "He has an apartment somewhere in Pleasantville."

"It's down at the edge of Main Street," Mark added. "Opposite end of the street from the school. The place looks like an old motel."

"I know it," said the officer. "What's his last name again?"

"Casterbridge, Jeremy Casterbridge," Mark replied. "Apartment three."

The lieutenant stared at Mark. "How do you know so much?"

"Kristy and I happened to browse Main Street today. Last night, Jeremy mentioned an apartment at the edge of town. We passed by the building, and it seemed an obvious place for him to be. We checked the names on the mailboxes and found his."

"And where were you folks tonight?"

Kristy answered. "DaVinci's, a restaurant a few miles outside of town. Pete was supposed to join us, but he never arrived," she finished softly.

O'Malley jotted down the name of the restaurant and stood.

"Mrs. Blakely, I'm very sorry for what's happened. Are you folks from around here?"

Kristy answered, "No, we're from New York City, but we're staying in the house."

O'Malley said, "Good. I wouldn't want you to be alone, Mrs. Blakely."

"Omigod. My daughter. Raven's with the babysitter. I have to go and get her."

"We'll go get her for you if you want, Erin," Kristy soothed.

"I'll be in touch with you tomorrow," O'Malley said. "We'll need your identification of the deceased and some kind of statement, but tomorrow's soon enough. You both will be here?"

"We were planning to leave in the morning," Kristy explained.

"I hope you'll put it off for an hour or two," the lieutenant suggested, in a way that meant they should plan on it. "I'll be happy to talk to you early and not hold you up too long. I'll call around nine. Will that suit?"

Kristy answered, "Yes."

"Let me have your names and addresses, just in case."

Mark and Kristy produced driver's licenses, and the lieutenant took what information he needed, along with their cell numbers.

The lieutenant approached two officers who stood at the front door, and Mark overheard the lieutenant direct them to Apartment 3. The two officers preceded O'Malley out the door.

"I can't believe it," Erin murmured, alone now with her two friends. She addressed Mark. "Please, don't leave tomorrow."

"My mom's expecting us," Kristy said in a low voice.

"Let's see how the morning goes," Mark added.

"Thank you. What do I do now? What?"

"Are you able to go and get Raven?" Kristy asked.

Erin took a deep breath. "Yes, let me wash my face. I'll have to tell her something, won't I? An accident. I can't tell her the man who came here last night, that he..." She rose and walked to the downstairs powder room.

"I tried to get us out of here," Kristy whispered after Erin disappeared.

"I know you did, but it seems a little callous to run out first chance after a thing like this."

"I know, I know."

"If there's an obvious opportunity to leave, if she offers it to us, though, let's agree now we'll take advantage of it."

"And if there isn't?"

"We'll do what I said—see how the morning goes. I guess one more day won't kill us. Oh, bad choice of words.

Erin entered the room. "I'll go to get Raven myself. I'll be fine. I may be a while with her. You don't have to sit up for me...or with me. I'll be fine."

"Are you sure you don't want some company?" Kristy asked.

Erin walked toward Kristy and Mark, and they both rose.

She embraced Kristy and said, "I'm so glad you're here—both of you. But no, I'd rather do this on my own. I'll be fine." She took Mark's hand in hers. "I'll see you in the morning." Erin stepped resolutely out of the front door and disappeared into the night.

"Very stiff upper lip," Mark said. "Now what do we do?"

Kristy considered. "I don't think we want to lock ourselves in our bedroom quite yet, do we? Want to drive back to DaVinci's? It had a nice little bar, and I could eat a bit more. I think I've recovered enough from the margarita."

Mark shrugged agreeably. "Beats walking up and down Main Street for the next couple of hours."

They rose and left the house quiet and deserted.

Six

"How's Raven taking all of this?" Kristy asked when Erin returned to the house after dropping the child at school the next morning. "More coffee, Mark?"

"Yes, thanks."

Kristy poured. "Erin?"

"Coffee? Yes, please." Erin slumped into a kitchen chair. "I find she's looking at me to figure out how she should react. If I keep a straight face, she does. Last night when I told her Pete had an accident, I teared up and so did she. This morning, I asked her whether she wanted to go to school today. Having an option seemed to puzzle her. I intend to keep her days as close to normal as I can. I just brushed her hair as always and took her to school."

Erin's voice faded as the phone rang, and she went to answer it.

Mark and Kristy heard Erin say, "Nine-thirty will be fine. Yes, they're here. I'll tell them." She hung up. "The police lieutenant. He wants me to identify the body, and he wants to talk to us."

Erin sat, lifted her coffee cup, but set it back down.

"I hope you'll both stay over one more day. I know your mom's expecting you. Maybe you can change her mind, Mark."

"I'm sure Kristy can give her mom a call." Kristy's and Mark's eyes locked for a brief, helpless moment.

Kristy smiled Erin's way. "Sure. You'll have a lot to get through today. What are friends for?"

"Thank you, Kristy. Thank you so much."

~ * ~

After their visit to the police station, Erin closeted herself with the town's funeral director. At Erin's insistence, Mark and Kristy went their own way, planning to meet for lunch after Erin completed her grim task. A bit later, Mark and Kristy found themselves seated on a bench in a small park off Main Street.

A large golden leaf dropped onto Kristy's lap from the trees above. She picked it up by the stem and idly twirled it.

"You were in with Lieutenant O'Malley at least half an hour," she said. "What was that all about? I was in and out in ten minutes."

Mark stretched his arm out and put it around Kristy's shoulders. He bent his head toward her and kissed her.

"You're not upset, I hope, about staying another day," he said.

"As long as we keep the hugging and kissing to a minimum," she said, giving him a look.

"You mean...?" He removed his arm from around Kristy and sat back.

"Funny man. I mean with Erin."

Mark snuggled closer. "She's in no state of mind to be hugging and kissing anyone."

"We were talking about you and the lieutenant," Kristy reminded him. "A long time together?"

"It wasn't so long."

Kristy sighed discontentedly.

"All right. All right. I asked him as many questions as he asked me."

"You're not getting snoopy again, are you? You know what happens when you get snoopy."

Mark and Kristy had undergone a brief but painful separation when, over her protests, Mark had chosen to look into the death of her brother. Mark's concern had proved valid, but they'd paid a steep price for the disruption to their lives.

"Just naturally curious. Anyway, who snooped over lunch the other day, asking about boyfriends and such?"

"Never mind that now. What did the police officer tell you?"

Mark gave a chuckle. "Oh, someone else is naturally curious, too?"

"What did you find out?" Kristy spoke the words with slow impatience.

"Somehow both of those men, Jeremy and Pete, ended up at the same restaurant last night."

"What? Where? Not DaVinci's. We were there."

"No, not DaVinci's. Ten minutes outside of town in the opposite direction from where we ate."

"How'd Pete end up there?"

Mark shrugged. "The restaurant is named DiVito's. You take it from there."

"He botched the names?"

"Could be. Or he somehow knew where to find Jeremy. Jeremy was at the bar when he arrived."

"And?"

"According to people in the restaurant, Pete approached Jeremy, and they started arguing."

"A spat? Physical?"

"No, not physical. Intense, though. The restaurant asked them both to leave."

"If Pete wondered where we were, why didn't he call...oh, her cell battery."

"Right, he couldn't. The two men left the restaurant within a few minutes of one another, and the rest is...mystery. Jeremy left first and admits going to Erin's house to look for her. He claims the house was dark. He waited a little while, and then went home. Somebody at the apartment house saw his lights on around nine o'clock. They didn't go on at nine o'clock. They were on when the person noticed at nine o'clock. So, no helpful information there."

"Jeremy, then, not only lacks a decent alibi, but places himself at the scene of the crime after having argued with the victim."

"That's about the size of it."

"Did they arrest him?"

"You bet they did. Somebody caved in Pete's head with a large rock from the garden. He was struck twice, so, unless he bounces, he didn't trip and fall."

"Does Erin know all of these details?"

"I don't know, but she won't hear any of it from me." Mark stood and stretched. "Walk a little?"

Kristy stood and took Mark's hand. "We're leaving in the morning, right?" she asked.

"Absolutely."

"No snooping? At least no more than you've already done."

"Think there's anything to snoop into?"

Kristy shook her head. "I don't, but I bet you could find something. Please don't. The police seem to have things well in hand."

"Yes, darling. But no more snooping from you, either. No more leading questions, please."

"Let's go see how Erin's getting along." Hand in hand, they made their way back to Quinn's Funeral Home two blocks off Main Street.

Erin walked slowly down the side pathway from the office entrance to Quinn's as Mark and Kristy approached.

Erin smiled weakly their way. "Just in time."

"Everything attended to?" Kristy asked.

"I think so. Sunday afternoon. The coffin will be closed. Well, you don't need to know all the gory details. Oh, and I know you have to be at the theatre on Sunday, so...so don't feel you need to make an appearance. Your staying today is what I really appreciate." They moved a few steps toward the end of town where they'd eaten lunch the day before. In a voice of suppressed anger, Erin said, "I hope they put Jeremy away for good this time."

"You really think he did this?" Mark asked.

Erin stood still a moment. When they continued on, she said, "The same thing happened with Lenny. An argument—Jeremy waited for him outside his building—a fight, or maybe not even a fight this time."

After a suitable pause, Mark said, "I don't see how he imagined ever getting away with it. He's an obvious suspect."

"He's very cocky. Anyone who knows him...and self-righteous. If he believes he's entitled to a thing or to do a thing, the rightness or wrongness of it doesn't enter into his calculations. His sense of entitlement takes precedence." In a softer voice, she said, "And he has a temper. Kristy has seen, it as I recall."

Kristy gave a nearly imperceptible nod. "You and he did get into it one night in the apartment. I mentioned a pip of an argument to you, Mark, but I don't think I really did justice to the violence...the verbal violence of it."

"I'm going to sell the house, and get the hell out of this town," said Erin. "Maybe I'll move to New York. Any acting spots available?"

"We always hire for specific plays," said Kristy.

Mark's stomach dropped. The look in Kristy's eyes told him she knew she'd spoken too quickly.

"It's something to think about," said Erin, and she began to discuss Kristy's and her work in *The Winter's Tale*.

Lunch and the rest of the day passed quietly. It surprised Mark how such a horrific act could occur and not leave behind it a thorough jumble of chaos and actions that needed to be taken. Other than the visits to the police and the funeral home, no such swirl of activity occurred.

They picked up an exceptionally quiet Raven, and with Raven in tow, the adults kept everything as normal as possible. Kristy cooked another spaghetti dinner. Raven finally fell asleep on the sofa while the adults chatted—her presence forcing them to keep the subject matter harmless—and by ten-thirty, everyone retired for the night. Raven did insist, though, on sleeping with her mother.

~ * ~

The next morning Kristy and Mark drove Erin and Raven to school—Erin said she would walk home—and by nine-thirty they sat in the kitchen of Kristy's mother's house in the town of Brunton, thirty miles away, having their second cups of coffee of the day.

Betty King, Kristy's mother, did not act as shocked as Mark expected at the news from Pleasantville.

"Oh, yes, I remember her very well. The girl who never wore enough clothing. Imagine how thrilled I was to learn such an uninhibited young lady was Kristy's roommate, Mark."

"She's a good person, Mom. A lot of fun."

"You see what a lot of 'fun' leads to."

"Can we change the subject?" Kristy groused.

They could, and they did. Mark avoided being alone with Betty, not wanting either of them to have an opportunity to mention their shared secret-to-the-grave past. In the afternoon, Kristy arranged for flowers to be sent to the funeral home, and in the evening, she and Mark took Betty to dinner. Late the next morning, Mark and Kristy were back at work in the theatre, relieved and grateful to be there.

Seven

Rehearsals for *Lady Windermere's Fan* took up where they had left off, and the play opened on schedule. The actors breathed sighs of relief and joy as the one hundred sixty opening-night patrons applauded energetically and sent the cast across the street to the opening-night party at Phebe's, the downtown actors' bar, in high spirits.

Kristy handed Mark a glass of red wine. "Well, that was fun, Lord W."

"It was indeed, Lady W." Mark sipped his wine. "You were very good. This is the first time we've really played opposite one another. We're a good team."

Kristy laughed. "Burton and Taylor."

"Thank goodness not Abbott and Costello. Are you positive she's coming?" Mark asked.

Kristy shrugged. "She promised. That's all I can tell you."

Erin had phoned Kristy a half-dozen times since the funeral. Kristy mentioned the opening-night party, and Erin angled for an invitation. Kristy offered the invitation as well as their living room sofa and held her breath. When Erin accepted the party invitation but declined the sofa, Kristy told Mark she felt a bit ashamed at feeling relieved.

"Speak of the devil," said Mark, looking over Kristy's shoulder. Erin, smiling as always, approached, her jacket folded over her arm. She wore a short black skirt and a frilly pink transparent peasant blouse, highlighted by the slender black bra beneath it. Erin pecked Kristy's cheek and moved to embrace Mark.

"I'm sorry I wasn't able to come to the play, but I was with real estate people until two hours ago. I went back to my hotel, cleaned up, and here I am." She spread her arms and grinned.

"Give me your jacket," Mark said. "White wine?" He took the jacket to the coat rack and brought back a glass of wine for Erin.

"I was telling Erin how well things came off tonight," Kristy said.

"This is so exciting, and I'm so jealous," Erin gushed. "I hope your offer for me to take up my acting career in your company is still good, but we'll talk about it later."

Erin filled in Mark and Kristy about the apartments she'd seen and her plans to settle in New York City.

"I'm going to take the two-bedroom in Battery Park City, and the sooner the better. I want out of Unpleasantville, and I detest all of this apartment hunting. The apartment's a quick cab ride to the theatre, too, in case you hire me." Erin put her hand on Mark's arm for a moment, leaned into him, and gave him her biggest smile. "Boss."

Marty Schonbaum, a retired English professor and frequent member of the acting troupe, took Mark away for a time. When Mark returned, Erin was bidding Kristy good-bye.

"I have to put a down payment on the apartment tomorrow, and then scoot back home to Raven, but we'll be New Yorkers soon. I'll call you." Erin hugged Kristy and kissed Mark on the lips. Mark avoided Kristy's eyes and retrieved Erin's jacket.

"She comes and goes like a whirlwind," said Mark.

"And this is the older version. Imagine."

"I don't doubt we'll be seeing more of her." Mark drained his glass. "Want another?"

"Yes, and let's go join the party. Happy nights like these are few and far between." She leaned forward quickly and kissed Mark on the lips.

"What's that for?"

"I like to be the woman who's most recently kissed you."

"Fine with me. By the way, you didn't see, but I brushed hers off when she wasn't looking. So you know."

"Pssshht," Kristy scoffed, walking off.

~ * ~

Four nights later, the phone rang in the apartment.

"I'm cooking, Mark. Get it, please," Kristy called from the kitchen.

AWB needed to select a play to follow *Lady Windermere*, and Mark had been looking over a list of possibilities. Fifteen minutes later, Kristy put dinner on the table: a combination of chicken, asparagus, and bean curd she'd stir-fried while Mark continued to chat on the phone. Kristy gestured imperatively to him, and a moment later he came to the table.

"What's up?" Kristy asked.

"Your friend."

"Erin?"

"None other."

"What'd she want? You?"

"She said 'hi,' by the way. I told her you were cooking. She's coming in a week from next Tuesday morning to do a reading. She wants a job, and she strongly suggests the next play we do is your old favorite."

"My old favorite?"

"*The Winter's Tale*. She says you and she would be a sensation."

"You invited her to try out?"

"Not exactly. She asked for it. I felt obligated to say yes. She's your friend. She's a new widow. She's moving to a new city and needs something to do. You did make this offer, you know, not me. Anyway, I felt obligated. I couldn't find any reason to say no."

They ate silently for a moment.

"Maybe she won't be any good."

"Ha! No chance," said Kristy. "She'll be very good. She's a natural."

Mark heard gloom in Kristy's voice. "She said she's already sold her house, and she and Raven move into the new apartment next Monday."

"And Tuesday she's coming to the theatre?"

"So she says."

"Doesn't waste any time, does she? I guess the appropriate thing is to have her and Raven for dinner Tuesday night."

"Your call."

"Any news about Jeremy? Is he still in jail? Can they prove he really murdered her husband?"

Mark spread his hands. "Topic didn't come up. Erin's conversation was all about Erin. Besides, you don't want me to pry, do you?" He lifted his eyebrows expectantly.

"No, *I don't* want you to pry." A few moments later, Kristy asked, "Want to take a walk after dinner? It's nice out."

"Good idea. I think I'd like some air."

~ * ~

Forty minutes later, Kristy and Mark walked hand in hand along Church Street in the cool and pleasant evening.

"Where shall we go?" Kristy leaned her head briefly on Mark's shoulder.

"Oh, how about over to Broadway, window shop a little, down to the Battery and back up Church Street?"

"Wow, a real man of decision. And ambitious, too. May I ask you a question?"

"You just did. You mean another one?"

"Funny. Were your parents happily married?"

Mark gave Kristy a look. "Where'd that come from?"

"Were they?"

"I suppose. I never noticed any particular tension. Nothing out of the ordinary. Of course, I moved out for the most part at eighteen—first to Cornell, and then here."

"They both died your first year in New York?"

"They did. Four months apart. Erin and I are both orphans of the storm."

"My father worked all the time." Kristy's late father had owned a liquor store and distributorship and made a great deal of money from them. "In my mind's eye, I always see my parents together dressed up, going somewhere or entertaining. Don't get me wrong. They always had time for my brother and me, especially my mom. I think Erin's lucky to have Raven, don't you? I see her devotion. Believe me, selflessness is a quality new to Erin."

Mark had wondered how this topic arose, and now he had a clue.

Kristy kept on with her train of thought. "Erin obviously wasn't happy being married. It used to always be about play with her—back when I knew her, I mean. She didn't take very much very seriously."

"I picked up on that in the sailor story, but she seems to take motherhood seriously."

"The first night in the kitchen while she cooked, she said having Raven was for real, and being married was for real."

"Raven's a real joy—marriage is real work, I suppose."

"You think being married spoils things?" Kristy trained her gaze on him.

"Some people think so."

"Who?"

"Comedians."

"Comedians," Kristy said dismissively.

"What do you give a woman to reduce her sex drive?"

Kristy sighed. "What?"

"A marriage license. And Oscar Wilde said something about marriage being the meal where the dessert is served first."

"There's more to marriage than sex," Kristy said brusquely and released Mark's hand.

"I guess there better be."

"You can't believe the nonsense you're spouting. You're trying to goad me."

Mark put his arm around Kristy's waist. "Are you proposing to me?"

Kristy ignored Mark's question. "It must be very special to have a Raven in your life. That's my point."

"Your point is well taken." They walked silently for a moment. "Somehow, things haven't been on an even keel since we set foot into Pleasantville. Erin seems to have a way of wriggling into places and sort of upsetting things—of sending the mind off to spots it wouldn't otherwise go."

"Mmm, like you admiring low-cut blouses and appreciating random hugs and kisses?"

Mark had been thinking about Erin, but not in that way. He wasn't yet prepared, though, to share any doubts about Erin with Kristy. "Don't be silly," he said.

"I don't know," Kristy said softly, adding a shrug. "Suppose she's really good at the reading next week. Want to do *The Winter's Tale*? I wouldn't mind. If we get the last scene, the statue scene, right, it's a beautiful piece of theatre."

"I've read the play over twice since you first mentioned it."

"So, you *have* been thinking about it?"

"Your friend would have to be extremely good. The scene you mentioned, where the statue comes alive, largely depends on her."

"I can play Paulina again."

Mark heard the excitement creeping into Kristy's tone.

"Let's see how she does at the reading," he cautioned.

"I want to be there."

"I wouldn't hold it without you, darling. We'll invite Tony, Karen, and Marty, too. You're certain, though, you want her around? She seems to..." Mark waggled his hand back and forth. "...disrupt things on occasion."

Kristy stretched up to kiss him. She took his arm from around her waist and held his hand.

"I'll rely on you to see that no disruptions occur."

Mark raised his right hand and said, "Won't be my fault if they do."

They continued down the street as Mark's mind returned to Pleasantville. He began carefully—and not for the first time—to go over every incident of their visit to Erin.

Eight

Hermione: How will this grieve you
When you shall come to clearer knowledge that
You thus have publish'd me! Gentle my lord,
You scarce can right me thoroughly then to say
You did mistake.

Leontes: No; if I mistake
In those foundations which I build upon,
The center is not big enough to bear
A schoolboy's top. Away with her to prison!
He who shall speak for her is afar off guilty
But that he speaks.

Kristy sat in an aisle seat in the third row of the Bouwerie Lane
Theatre. Tony Babbitte and Karen Christenson, permanent members
of the AWB troupe, and Marty Schonbaum sat across the aisle from

her. Mark and Erin sat at a wooden table on stage reading from *The Winter's Tale*.

Hermione: Do not weep, good fools;
There is no cause: when you shall know your mistress
Has deserv'd prison, then abound in tears
As I come out: this action I now go on
Is for my better grace. Adieu, my lord:
I never wish'd to see you sorry; now
I trust I shall. My women, come; you have leave.
Leontes: Go, do our bidding: hence!

Erin closed her copy of the play and looked expectantly out into the audience.

Tony, Karen, and Marty struck up applause, and Kristy, who could not keep from smiling, joined in.

On stage, Mark extended his hand to Erin and shook it. "Fabulous."

Kristy leapt up the two feet to the stage followed by Tony, Karen, and Marty.

Kristy took Mark's arm. "Didn't I say she was a natural?"

"You did. You did. Very impressive, Erin."

The other actors offered their congratulations.

Tony said, "You'll do Leontes, Mark. You haven't played a big Shakespeare role in a while. Me, Florizel, Polixenes, Autolycus? What do you think?"

"Your call. But we seemed to have reached a decision. Shakespeare it will be then?"

"The old shepherd for me," said Marty, rubbing his hand over his trim beard.

"Perdita?" Mark asked, looking at Karen.

"The love interest. Type-cast again." Everyone laughed.

"I'll ask Barbara to put out a casting call for next Monday at ten, and we'll be off. Everybody's free then, right?" Barbara was Barbara Gray, AWB's business manager, an older woman from an empty nest who enjoyed being around the theatre.

The actors offered Erin one last round of handshakes and dispersed, leaving Mark, Kristy, and Erin on stage.

"I enjoyed the reading so much. I'm relieved you liked it."

"I'll go hunt up Barbara," said Mark. "See you tonight, Erin."

"I'm glad we read early," said Erin, following Kristy backstage and down the stairs to the basement exit. She opened the door. "I can spend the rest of the day getting the apartment in order. Raven's already in P. S. 243, so I can work like a maniac until two-thirty. We'll both see you tonight."

~ * ~

A few minutes past six o'clock, Mark welcomed Erin and Raven. Erin had changed from the discreet brown turtleneck and tan slacks she'd worn at the reading to a white halter, a plaid skirt that ended mid-thigh, and red high heels. Raven toted a few picture books under her arm, her lustrous black hair tied back out of the way.

"Hello, Raven." Mark put his hand atop the child's head for a moment. "It's nice to see you again."

"We live in the Big Apple now," Raven explained. "Batry City. In an apartment. I have my own room, and I see the Statue of Liverdy out my window."

"Congratulations," said Kristy, handing Erin a glass of red wine and gesturing to the cluster of a sofa and some chairs in the living room. "They have nice playgrounds over there."

"We went to one after school today. The floor is all sand," Raven reported.

Erin took a seat on the sofa, making no effort to control the rise of her skirt. She smiled proudly as she listened to Raven's conversation.

"How's your new school?" Mark asked. "What's your teacher's name?"

"Miss Elizabeth. She's pretty."

"Lucky you."

"I brought books." Raven extended her stash toward Mark.

Mark dutifully inspected them.

"Can I go over there?" Raven pointed toward the window.

"By all means," Kristy answered. "Let me get the light for you."

"So, are you settled in somewhat?" Mark asked.

"It'll be a while, but even I like looking out the window and seeing the Statue of Liverdy." They glanced at Raven, deep into her books.

Kristy lowered her voice. "Have you heard anything from Pleasantville? I mean about Jeremy?"

"As of yesterday, he was still in jail, and the investigation continues, according to Lieutenant O'Malley. I don't know what there is to investigate. It's all so obvious."

"The police still need concrete evidence to tie him to the murder." Mark stopped short, wondering how the word 'murder' would affect Erin.

"I guess," was all she said.

"What about determining Raven's father?" Kristy asked quietly.

Erin shook her head slightly and shrugged. "Do I really want to know? Raven is simply Raven to me—a creature precious and entire in herself. She's mine, and the fathering is irrelevant, at least as far as I'm concerned. Besides, Jeremy's going away for a good long time, maybe forever. I hope any future involvement in my life will become a moot point."

"I hope it all works out for you," Kristy said earnestly. "I really do."

"Don't worry about me. I know how to get by. Oh, before I forget." She opened her purse, reached inside, and produced a postcard. "I picked this up in the lobby of my building."

She passed the postcard to Kristy. "You don't play Wednesday nights, right?"

"No, we don't," Mark answered, studying Erin carefully for a moment. "Thursday through Sunday afternoon. What is it?"

"An art opening." Kristy handed Mark the card.

"It's tomorrow night," Erin explained.

Mark gave Erin a quizzical look. "Shoko Takeda. The art of the crane?"

Erin gave a laugh. "What's the difference? Let's catch an art opening, and then I'll take you to dinner to thank you for all you've done. There's a great French restaurant, Felix, almost across the street from the Agora Gallery over on West Broadway. Walking distance for you two. I'll take a cab and meet you. Six-thirty okay?"

Kristy cast Mark a questioning glance. "Okay with you?"

"Sure, why not?" Mark agreed. "Raven coming along?"

"No, no. I already have a nice high-school girl—same floor as me—lined up for babysitting."

"Dinner should be ready by now," said Kristy. "Is everyone ready for filet mignon, garlic mashed potatoes, and asparagus?"

Raven rose from the floor and joined the adults.

"What's that?" Raven asked.

"What's what, honey?" Erin answered.

"The filly thing."

Kristy explained. "Filet mignon. It's beef, but I made a hamburger and French fries for you. I thought you'd like it better."

"Yes!" said Raven, gesturing with her tiny fist.

The grown-ups laughed, and Kristy led everyone into the kitchen for dinner.

Nine

When Mark and Kristy arrived at the Agora Gallery, Erin greeted them, tiny plastic cup of red wine in one hand, a half-dozen papers stapled together in the other. The entrance to the fifth floor gallery led along a counter covered with cups filled with either red or white wine. To the left, the gallery spread wide into four large, open rooms through which people meandered, examining the art on the walls.

Erin gestured toward the countertop, and Mark picked up a red wine and a white wine. He and Kristy joined Erin in the middle of the front room. Erin dressed, as usual, in a manner emphasizing her assets to any interested eye. Tonight, she wore tight black slacks and an abbreviated black tank top with an inch or two of torso in view, along with black high heels.

"So where is the illustrious Mr. or Ms. Takeda?" Mark asked.

"It's a group show. I didn't know. Hard to tell who's an artist and who isn't."

Mark scanned the walls of the gallery and saw so many styles on exhibit he knew they could not possibly be the work of one person. "I don't see the cranes. Shall we go find them?"

Erin studied the papers in her hand a moment and said, "Room three. Follow me." She led the way toward the back of the gallery and veered off into a smaller room on the left. Four drawings of cranes hung on one wall of the room.

Erin studied her papers. "Pencil on paper. Four hundred fifty dollars each. Take one home?" she asked with a smile. "Here, see what else they have." She handed the papers to Mark.

Mark wandered off alone, content to leave Erin to Kristy. Each artist had contributed a handful of pieces, and standing amid the clusters of people inspecting each artist's work stood one person, eyes eager and hopeful—the artist.

Mark chose one exhibit and studied it—four collages of brassy metallic pieces put together into random shapes on a white background. On closer inspection, he realized the collages were merely paper treated and formed to look like metal.

"They caught my eye, too." He heard Erin's voice at his elbow. "Good, aren't they?"

"Very striking, I must say." He studied the papers in his hand. "Six hundred fifty bucks a pop."

"I'm glad you like them," came a second voice. A man about thirty, dressed in jeans and a blue, buttoned shirt stood behind Mark. Slightly taller than Mark, he sported an artistically long mane of light brown hair.

"Are you the artist?" Erin asked.

The man gave a slight bow of the head.

"I was saying your work is very striking," said Mark.

"Thank you. Thank you very much. Each piece takes two weeks to complete. So you see two months of my life before you,"

Kristy slipped her arm through Mark's, and Mark instantly felt more comfortable.

"Is this how you make your living?" Mark asked and sipped his wine.

"I wish. No, I'm actually a photographer. Until recently, I worked out of a studio about an hour and a half from here. A small town in Pennsylvania, Galloway by name."

"You must be kidding," Erin burst in. "That's like three miles from Pleasantville."

"You know Pleasantville?" the artist asked in surprise.

"I do. I just moved from there—this week, in fact—to Battery Park City."

"Really! I've recently moved into the city myself—into a loft over near the Williamsburg Bridge. Fifteen Dunham Place. Nothing like Battery Park City, though. Oh, excuse me. The gallery people." He whispered the last words, and moved off to speak with a young, petite, very attractive Asian woman, who introduced him to a pair of well-dressed matrons.

"I can't believe he's from around Pleasantville," Erin said. "Go figure. What's his name? Oh, I see on the wall. Bob Collins. His stuff is very nice, don't you think?" She examined the pieces more closely while Mark and Kristy wandered off.

"Serendipitous," Kristy remarked.

"Really. Can't get away from Pleasantville, no matter how we try. Does he look familiar to you?"

Kristy shook her head. "Getting a case of *déjà vu*?"

"I don't know what I'm getting. Except another glass...cup...children's-sized portion...of wine. Want one?"

"I'll come." Kristy followed Mark to the service table. Wine in hand, they browsed the art for another twenty minutes before returning to the front of the gallery where the collages hung. There, they saw Erin still in conversation with the artist, who immediately moved off toward the front counter.

"I sent Bob off to get me another wine."

"Bob?" Kristy said, shooting one eyebrow skyward.

Erin winked. "My new friend Bob. Tracy thinks she may have sold two of his pieces."

"Tracy?" Mark asked.

"The gallery woman who took him away a while ago. He can't have dinner with us tonight—he has to be here until the opening closes." She giggled. "Opening closes. Silly. But he said he'd be happy to meet us for a drink around eight-thirty across the way at Felix."

"He doesn't waste time," Kristy commented.

"Somebody doesn't," Mark mumbled.

"Let's take one last look around, and we'll go have our dinner."

Bob walked up and handed Erin her plastic cup. "I have to go make nice," he said, then rejoined Tracy, who still chatted with the same two matronly women.

~ * ~

Shortly after eight-thirty, Bob entered the restaurant. Erin had seated herself with an eye poised to watch the entrance, and as soon as Bob appeared, she rose and waved to him.

"How'd it go? Did you make your sale?" Erin poured some red wine from the bottle on the table into Bob's glass.

"It looks like I did. Now, I only hope Mrs. Clifford and Mrs. Gettison show me off to their rich friends, and the orders start pouring in."

"Order something to eat," Erin suggested.

"I'll just get a couple of appetizers. That won't take so long."

Bob contributed nothing to the conversation as he ate. When the waiter removed his plate, Mark asked him, "Have you sold many pieces?"

"It's not an easy thing to do. Buying art doesn't appear high on the agenda of too many people, nowadays. I've made a couple sales in my time, but making art has to be something you do because you like to, not because you need the money."

"I can understand that," Mark concurred.

"Mark writes fiction," Kristy bragged.

"Any luck there?" Bob asked.

"A few stories published."

"He's working on a murder mystery novel," Kristy chirped proudly.

"Murder mystery!"

"He's very good at solving things, aren't you, darling?"

Mark gave a small shrug and listened as Kristy recounted the adventures of the AWB Theatre Company, and the murders of its two founding members—murders Mark helped solve.

Mark was not surprised when she omitted the investigation which put so much strain on their relationship—his investigation into the murder of her brother.

"The book he's working on tells the story of the first murder at AWB, when we put on *Hamlet*. Or tried to, anyway," Kristy concluded.

"I'll look forward to reading it one day," Bob promised. "Well, I have to get going. I have a ton of stuff to do tomorrow."

"I'd better go, too," Erin interjected. "My babysitter has school tomorrow. Big history test, she tells me. Shall we share a cab?"

"Let's."

Erin stood. "I'll get the waiter."

The bill paid, Erin and Bob said their good-byes and left.

Mark emptied the rest of the wine into his and Kristy's glasses. "What do you think?"

"About?"

"Erin seems to have gotten over her recent loss without much heartbreak."

Kristy shrugged. "She and Pete weren't getting along much, anyway." She stared into Mark's eyes. "There's something on your mind. I know the look, and I'm afraid to ask what it is."

Mark smiled and took Kristy's hand. "I won't bother you with it until I know the something on my mind is really a something."

"What are you thinking about?" Kristy asked in a leery voice.

"I'm going to take a little walk tomorrow morning. You're welcome to come along if you want."

"Where are you going?"

"To take a look at the building where Erin lives. You have her address, right?"

"I do. What are you looking for?"

"Now, now. You're afraid to ask, remember?"

"Maybe I will go with you."

Mark lifted his wine glass and indicated Kristy should do the same.

"It's a date," he said, and they touched glasses. They finished off their wine and stepped out into the cool night air. They said very little on the walk home, both wondering what their next day's morning walk would tell them.

Ten

Battery Park City was a residential enclave built out into the Hudson River from landfill created by the construction of the World Trade Center, and it had become a small city unto itself. Apartment buildings, businesses, schools, banks, a cinema, bus service, supermarkets, parks, a theatre—a person could stay in Battery Park City a long time without ever having to leave.

In the crisp air, under a cloudless sky, Mark and Kristy strolled hand in hand along the river esplanade toward Erin's building. Mark knew Kristy was dying to know the purpose of their reconnaissance, but he wanted Kristy to ask before he offered an explanation. After the way she had blown up and stormed out on him when he said he planned to investigate the death of her brother, he didn't know how she'd take his prying into the life of her friend.

Kristy pointed at a high-rise building overlooking the harbor. "She lives there."

"Two bedrooms?"

"That's what she told me."

"Must've cost a pretty penny."

"She got a ton of money from selling her house, plus life insurance, plus the car business, plus a bank account. What are we looking for? You've been very close-mouthed, and I know you've been waiting for me to ask you what's up."

Mark laughed. "We know each other too well. We're looking for more postcards."

"Postcards?"

"Like the one Erin pulled from her pocketbook announcing the opening."

"Why?"

"You'll see. I think."

They entered the spacious lobby of the building. A uniformed guard behind a desk greeted them.

"May I help you?"

Mark approached the guard's desk. "Yes. A friend of mine gave me a postcard—an announcement of an art opening. She said she picked it up here in the lobby. I wanted to get another one."

"Picked it up here?" The guard shook his head. "We don't allow circulars, menus, anything like that to clutter up the place. Look around."

The lobby was spare and clean. A square of four leather sofas outlined an area rug on one side of the guard's desk, and the mailboxes for the building were in an alcove on the other side. Potted greenery broke up the monotony of the open space.

"I see. Okay, thanks." Mark took Kristy by the hand and left the building.

Once outside, Kristy noticed an expectant twinkle in Mark's eye. "Okay, okay. What are we to take away from the fact there are no postcards? And how did you know there wouldn't be?"

"I didn't know. The gallery is an awfully long way from here for the building to offer postcards announcing its openings. Possible, but not likely, unless the crane painter lived here. I didn't expect we'd find it impossible for Erin to have picked up the postcard here. Erin said she picked up the postcard in the lobby of her building, didn't she? You heard her?"

"I heard her."

"Over there. Let's look in the supermarket. Maybe they have community news handouts, and Erin actually meant near her building."

The supermarket had a neighborhood bulletin board, but no collection of fliers or postcards announcing art gallery openings.

Mark and Kristy continued on in silence back toward the river esplanade.

Finally, Kristy said, "You want me to say she lied to us, don't you?"

"Didn't she?"

Kristy shrugged. "Okay, it doesn't seem like the postcard came from her lobby. She picked it up somewhere else. So? Maybe somebody gave it to her in the lobby. Is it important in some way?"

"I don't know. She got the postcard somewhere—from someone— but told us from her lobby, not from someone in her lobby. She wanted us to go to the opening with her. That's what the postcard was about. Why?"

Mark waited for Kristy to come up with an answer, but she maintained a stubborn silence for a moment. "You tell me."

"She wanted us to see her meet the collage-maker, Bob Collins. Didn't you find their meeting a bit forced?" Sarcasm tinged Mark's voice.

"Maybe. Why, though?"

"This kept me awake an extra hour last night, but I think it must have something to do with his being from her neighborhood back home."

Kristy's stubbornness lessened. "What's so important about his being from the next town over from Pleasantville?"

"I have work to do at the theatre most of today and tomorrow afternoon, and we're playing *Windermere* both nights, so we have no free time. Want to take a ride Saturday morning? Will the family purse bear the expense of renting a car for a few hours?"

"It will. Where are we going, and what are we looking for?"

"To Pleasantville, and do you really want to know?"

Kristy pondered a moment. "Yes."

"We're going to research our photographer slash collagist, Mr. Bob Collins. I can't figure why your friend would go to so much trouble to arrange that charade of meeting him in front of us."

"What do you want to find out about him?"

Mark shrugged. "Nothing specific. Whatever we can. There's a cab."

Kristy waved down the cab, and she and Mark climbed in.

"Bowery and Bond Streets," Mark told the driver. He bent his head toward Kristy. "I'm curious about him; aren't you?"

"It's a long way to drive to satisfy your curiosity."

Mark spread his palms, a gesture of helplessness. "It's the way my mind works."

"You and your mind. You really think Erin needs to be pried into, don't you?"

"The possibility did cross my mind. You must agree, she's going to odd lengths to do some odd things. If you'd like, we'll stop in and say hello to your mother on the way home. There should be enough time."

"You don't have to bribe me. I reluctantly acknowledge you sometimes know what you're doing."

"Damned with faint praise." He and Kristy rode the rest of the way to the Bouwerie Lane Theatre in silence.

~ * ~

Mark, in the driver's seat, and Kristy were on their way to Pleasantville by eight-thirty Saturday morning.

"Happy you picked *The Winter's Tale*?" Kristy asked, wondering whether she'd forced Mark and the theatre into something they would regret.

"Absolutely. Marty and I are already working on the staging. He'll get director's credit. He's very good. And you already know we have actors coming in on Monday to try out."

"Good." A moment later she asked, "Have you decided what it is we're looking for today?"

"Nope. At the moment, we're simply out for a drive on a nice autumn day. There'll probably be some color left in the trees. Care for some Brandi Carlile?"

Mark slid a CD into the dashboard slot, and Kristy leaned back and closed her eyes.

Ninety minutes later, Mark pulled over on the outskirts of Galloway. The change in the car's motion awoke Kristy.

"Are we there? Where are we?" She sat up and looked around.

"Galloway."

"Oh. Now what?"

"The town seems to do all of its business along Main Street. It looks residential beyond that. Let's drive along, and you look on the right for a photography studio. I'll search my side."

The stores along Main Street ran for ten blocks. When they reached the far end of town, Mark pulled over again.

"So, two of them?" he said.

"Yep, two.

"Now we take a closer look at them."

"Bob said he already closed up his studio."

"Won't matter. If there were three photo shops, the two we saw would know about the third. I don't see why a town this size would need three, though. Or even two, for that matter."

Mark made a U-turn and drove to the first photo shop, Ideal Photos. He parked the car, and he and Kristy went inside.

Mark addressed the clerk. "Hi, I'm looking for Bob Collins."

The clerk gave him a puzzled look. "I don't know any Bob Collins."

"He told us he ran a photo studio in Galloway."

The clerk shook his head. "There's only us and Mabel Chau's place six blocks down. No Bob Collins here, and certainly none there."

"That's odd. Thanks, though. You say six blocks down?"

"Mabel Chau's. Glorious Photo."

Mark and Kristy drove the six blocks, parked, and entered Glorious Photo. An Asian woman was puttering around the shelves arranging frames and samples of her work.

"Hi, are you Ms. Chau?"

"Mabel. Yes." The woman, no more than thirty, short and stocky, smiled and wiped her hands on her jeans. She'd tied her black hair into a ponytail.

"I'm looking for a photo studio run by a friend of mine, Bob Collins."

Mabel shook her head. "It's not in Galloway. Louis and I are the only two competing for the smiling faces of Galloway. Louis's place is a couple blocks down."

"Yes, we stopped there. Could there be a place on another street in Galloway?"

Mabel shook her head again. "All the stores are on Main Street except for the supermarket."

"What do you make of it?" Mark asked.

"You've got me," Kristy answered genuinely perplexed.

"Could it be on the road into town?"

"Could be anywhere, but it's not in Galloway."

"Well, thanks anyway." He and Kristy left the store and passed silently by a few storefronts before pausing.

"What do we do now?" Kristy asked.

"Why would he make up such a blatant lie?" Mark muttered.

"Hey!" Kristy said, brightening. "The local paper. If his studio's here, he probably advertises in the local paper. Brunton has a weekly... most small towns do."

"Well done, Watson. Let's go find one."

After a brief walk, Kristy pointed through the window of a real estate office. She entered and took a paper, *The Journal*, from a pile of a dozen.

"Here you go. The current edition." She handed the paper to Mark, who took it and paged slowly through it.

"Nothing. I see ads for Ideal Photo and Glorious Photo. No other photography stores, though."

"We should probably look in back issues. He wouldn't continue to advertise once he's left the place."

"Right. We need a back issue. Does this place have a library?"

"Let me go back in and ask." A moment later, Kristy returned and said, "Around the corner, two blocks down. Pioneer Street."

"Let's go, darling."

"Walking?"

"Walking. It's a beautiful day." The Galloway Library was a red brick building fronted by a leaf-covered lawn. Mark and Kristy crunched the dead leaves underfoot as they passed along the cement path to the steps leading up to the front door. Inside, the adult book room lay to the right, the children's room to the left.

"I'll ask at the desk," Mark said.

An auburn-haired woman of around fifty smiled at Mark. "May I help you?"

"Yes. Do you have back issues of *The Journal*?"

She pointed to the right wall. "In the cubbies over there—should be at least four months back."

Mark thanked the woman, and he and Kristy walked to where she'd indicated.

Kristy pulled out the stack of *The Journals*.

"Try the oldest one," Mark said.

Kristy handed him the bottom paper, and Mark leafed through it. Kristy took the next paper up and did the same.

"Bingo!" Mark cried softly when he reached page fourteen. "Artistic Photography. Here, look."

"There's his name. Bob Collins. But the studio's in Pleasantville."

"So it is. Looks like 'Artistic Photography Bob' lied to us, too."

"Four-seventeen Main Street."

"Shall we?"

"No doubt we shall." They replaced the newspapers, and Kristy accompanied Mark out the door and back to their car. As they drove, Mark asked, "Shall we have lunch in Pleasantville or is your mother expecting to feed us?"

"I told her we'd be there for lunch."

"Good. I don't want to spend more time than we have to in good old Pleasantville."

When they entered Pleasantville, Mark drove slowly, and Kristy checked the building addresses.

"Should be on the next block," said Kristy.

The 400 block of Main Street proved to be the block across from the school where they'd met Erin for lunch. Mark and Kristy followed the numbers.

Kristy pointed. "There's four-seventeen."

"Well, what do you know?"

"Isn't that the doorway where Erin said good-bye to someone?"

"And it's the building she went into the first day we came to pick up Raven," Mark added. "Oh!"

"What?"

"I think I know where I may have seen Mr. Bob Collins before— the fellow who looked into the car. He went into this building, remember?"

"Yes. Are you sure this is the building?"

"I am."

"And you're sure it was Bob?"

"I'm almost certain. He seemed familiar to me at the opening. I knew I'd seen him somewhere. Let's go in."

They entered the small lobby of the building. A one-foot square directory hung on the wall.

"He's still listed," Kristy said. "Third floor."

The stairway stood against the back wall of the lobby, and Mark and Kristy climbed two floors higher. There were two offices per floor in the four-story building. On the left as they came out of the staircase was Acme Insurance. On the right, the sign on the door read Artistic Photography. Mark tried the knob.

"Locked." He bent over and picked up three pieces of junk mail from the floor, one addressed to Bob Collins.

Kristy took one of the two remaining business cards from a clear plastic holder on the wall next to the door and handed it to Mark.

"Artistic Photography, Bob Collins," Mark read, and he slipped the card into the back pocket of his jeans.

Kristy opened the door to Acme Insurance, and she and Mark stepped inside. She smiled pleasantly at the young woman behind the desk and said, "Has the photography studio closed?"

"Yes. A couple weeks ago. I don't know what's going in there next."

"Thanks."

Kristy and Mark took the stairs to the street and stood for a moment in front of the building.

"So, what do you think?" Mark asked.

"You tell me."

"I think Erin knew Bob Collins while she lived in Pleasantville, and for some reason, she felt the need to enact the charming drama of meeting him at the opening. Don't you?"

Kristy nodded slowly. "I thought she was going to tell me about another man the night we talked in the kitchen—the night Jeremy showed up, but she didn't get a chance, and next day at lunch, you heard her deny it."

"Well, either you read her wrong, or she changed her mind about telling you."

"We're not going to let on to Erin we made this trip, are we?"

"No, but I guess it's good to know your friend is a consummate actress on a number of different levels."

"For some reason, I feel depressed knowing that."

"It probably doesn't concern us. We don't need to see the two of them together if we can somehow avoid it, but don't be surprised when your friend, Erin, comes bubbling to you about how wonderful the man she met at the opening is."

"Stop calling her my friend."

The visit to Brunton to see Kristy's mom proved painless enough for Mark, and on the trip home he refrained from raising the topic of Erin and her new friend.

Eleven

Lady Windermere played to a sold-out house on Saturday night, and when Kristy and Mark reached home after celebratory glasses of wine at Phebe's, they found a message from Erin on their answering machine.

"Hey, you guys. Did it go well tonight? Listen, I need a babysitter tomorrow afternoon and evening. Can I drop Raven at the theatre around four-thirty? You finish your matinee by then, don't you? Bob is taking me out. Give me a call anytime tonight until twelve-thirty."

Mark and Kristy exchanged looks.

"I think I mentioned bubbling," Mark said with a wry smile. "She sounded bubbly to me."

Kristy yawned. "She's probably embarrassed to let us know she fooled around with Bob back in Pleasantville."

Mark's eyebrows rose. "Embarrassed? Your friend? Excuse me. Your classmate, Erin?"

"Anything's possible. I'll give her a quick call. I'm sleepy."

Kristy called and accepted the babysitting assignment, and after she and Mark capped off the evening with one final, small glass of wine, they went to bed.

~ * ~

The next afternoon, Erin and Raven showed up outside the dressing rooms in the basement of the theatre as Mark and Kristy changed back into street clothes.

"Thanks, Kristy. This is a big help."

Kristy greeted the little girl. "Hello, Raven."

"Hey, kid," Mark joined in. "May I shake your hand?"

Raven extended her hand. Mark took it by the wrist and flopped her hand up down. "There, now I've shaken your hand."

Raven smiled uncertainly at her mother and then giggled.

"Here. Want to shake my hand?" Mark stretched out his arm, and Raven wrapped her two hands around his wrist and pumped up and down. Mark let his hand bounce freely. "Now that we've shaken each other's hands, shall we go to the playground?"

Raven nodded enthusiastically, and grasped Mark's extended hand. Together they approached the basement door.

"Take as long as you want," Kristy said to Erin. "Raven will be no trouble. Mark stepped out this morning and came home with a *Wizard of Oz* DVD to watch with her. I think he likes her."

"Seems so."

Out on the sidewalk, Mark and Kristy jumped into one cab with Raven in tow, and Erin got into another. Mark told the driver to head to Chinatown.

Columbus Park takes up two blocks in Chinatown and, at the south end, has an assortment of swings and climbing toys.

"Find a bench and relax," Mark said to Kristy. "I'll take the first shift. Come on, kid. I want to teach you something."

Kristy sat on a park bench in the gathering gloom and watched Mark lead Raven to the swings.

"You like to go high?" Mark asked.

Raven extended her arms toward Mark so he could lift her into the safety seat of the swing. Mark stood behind her and lifted the swing so Raven's ear was even with his mouth.

Kristy left her seat.

Mark whispered, "Raven, I want you to remember; the first swing is always the best. Can you remember?"

"Yes," Raven answered with enthusiasm.

"Say it to me," Mark demanded.

"The first swing is the best."

"Right. Ready?"

Raven's eyes widened.

Mark lifted the swing as high as he could. "One, two, here comes the first one!" He let go of the swing, and Raven gave a scream. Kristy laughed and joined Mark in pushing the swing.

"Higher," Raven cried.

"Thrill seeker."

"Like her mother," Kristy agreed.

After Raven tired of the swing, Mark chased her over and around the climbing toys until darkness put an end to the game.

"Do you like Chinese food?" Mark asked.

Raven shrugged. "What is it?"

"You know. Birds' beaks, pig bellies, cow tail, snake skin. Good things like that."

Raven's face clouded over like the sky before a squall.

"Just kidding," Mark cried. "You'll like it. It's all regular stuff. Promise. Ladies." Mark led the way to Mott Street, a block off, Raven eying him suspiciously.

By seven-thirty, they were back in the apartment seated on the sofa, a bowl of popcorn between them, ready to watch *The Wizard of Oz*. At nine-forty-five, their buzzer announced the return of Erin, who went straight to her daughter.

"Did you have a nice time, sweetheart?"

"We played swing and ate egg rolls—the kind without the bird beaks in them—and watched *Wizard of Oz*. The lion was funny!"

"No bird beaks and a funny lion. Great! Sounds like fun. I gotta go. Bob's holding the cab. Thanks a lot."

Erin took Raven's hand and, listening to a detailed report from Raven on her afternoon, hurried her from the apartment.

Mark sighed. "I'm pooped. Let's go to bed."

After quick showers, he and Kristy cuddled under the blankets, facing one another.

Kristy kissed Mark and said, "You're very good with children."

Mark shook his head with resolve. "If you'd seen me as a substitute teacher trying to teach English to junior-high students amidst the chaos of their delirium over the absence of their regular teacher, you would not say that. I would rather help Hercules clean out those stables with my bare hands before going back to substitute teaching again."

Kristy laughed. "Well, you won't have to. You're good with child. May I say that?"

Mark considered. "Maybe. One child. Small. Helpless. Totally unable to render me any physical harm and having no interest in cursing my mother."

"Don't pooh-pooh me. You were very good with Raven." Her voice softened further. "I'm proud of you. Did you ever imagine what it would be like to have one of your very own?"

Mark felt a nervous flutter. "Let's go to sleep."

"No, not until you acknowledge you were very good with Raven. Be a man and acknowledge it." Kristy moved her hand down Mark's stomach and took gentle hold of him. "If you do, I'll acknowledge how much of a man you really are."

Mark closed his eyes in stubbornness. "I will not. I will not," he muttered.

"Your top half is being stubborn, but your bottom half is giving way," Kristy whispered.

"Hard to fool you, eh?"

"Hard? Was that a pun? Say it."

In a soft voice, Mark said, "I got along very well with Raven."

"And one day you might like to have one of your very own."

"And one day you might like to have one of your very own. Ow! One day I might like to have one of my very own. Okay?"

The conversation ceased, and Kristy proved herself a woman of her word.

Twelve

O miserable lady! But, for me,
What case stand I in? I must be the poisoner
Of good Polixenes; and my ground to do't
Is the obedience to a master; one
Who, in rebellion with himself, will have
All that are his so too. To do this deed
Promotion follows.

A week later, on Monday morning at ten, the tryouts for *The Winter's Tale* began. Candidates offered favorite soliloquies and read specific passages from the play. At one o'clock, the AWB main players broke for lunch, planning to reassemble afterward to decide which actors to either call back or offer parts to.

Kristy, Erin, and Mark walked two blocks to Phebe's while the other members of the troupe opted for sandwiches from the local deli.

"This is so wonderful," Erin said excitedly after the waiter took their order. "I can't believe I'm really in New York City and about to be in a play. This is what I wanted back in Boston and for all of the time since then, Kristy."

Erin's exuberant rush of conversation prevented Kristy from responding.

"Raven is happy in her new school, and it's a miracle I happened across someone like Bob so quickly. It's like a dream come true."

Mark and Kristy fought the urge to look at one another.

"I'm really happy things are going your way," Kristy said. "Especially after everything that happened in Pleasantville."

A muted tune came from Erin's purse. She took out her phone and put it to her ear. "Hello." A look of horror came over her.

Mark and Kristy couldn't help but share a glance.

"How...how can this happen?" Erin stuttered vacantly. She closed her cell phone and faced the restaurant door.

"What's wrong?" Kristy asked. She and Mark both followed Erin's stare, and into the restaurant walked Jeremy.

"Good afternoon. I was outside the theatre and saw you come in here. I wanted a chance to speak with Erin, and I called to take away some of the shock of seeing me."

"Why are you here? What are you doing here?" Erin demanded.

Mark watched Erin and felt the fear in her eyes envelop the moment.

Jeremy pulled out the fourth chair and sat down.

"The police in Pleasantville are convinced they do not have a case against me. The reason, Erin, darling, is I had nothing to do with the death of your husband, but I think you know that."

"What are you talking about? How could they release you? You're a killer. You've killed before."

Mark extended his hand to suggest calm. "A restaurant is not the place for a conversation this enthusiastic."

"I'm fine," Jeremy said, making his own gesture to indicate both his calmness and reasonableness. "I've had a month or so to accustom myself to the situation. Captain Rufus Buttwad of the Pleasantville police finally saw his way clear to releasing me only a week ago. I've been living with my parents since then, trying to track you down, and now I have. I wanted to share the good news with you, Erin. I knew you'd be interested...happy for me?"

"It's not good news. How can they let you get away with this?"

"No, I'm not going to let you get away with this." Suddenly, Jeremy's eyes narrowed, and his voice hardened. "I know what you tried to do to me, Erin. It didn't take very long for me to piece it all together, but so far, I've kept it to myself. Be assured, though, I'll deal with it in my own way."

"What do you mean?" Erin challenged.

"I want to see my daughter, and I don't want anything you did in Pleasantville to muck it up. If it takes going through the courts to set up something legal and binding, I'll do it. I'd prefer we work something out together, though. It'll be quicker and cheaper."

"I'm not working out anything with you, you...you murderer. I don't need the police to tell me what you're like. I know what you're like. I know you, and I'm not having you around my daughter."

"Our daughter."

"No, my daughter."

"She is our daughter, and I want to see her."

"She is not your daughter. She is not." Erin set her jaw and then spat it out. "She's Lenny's child. Lenny is her father. Not you. Lenny and I were lovers when she was conceived. She is not yours." Erin rose from her seat. "I don't care what you do or what you say or what you threaten. She is my daughter, and you will never have her because she isn't your daughter." She started to leave.

Jeremy rose from his seat and grasped her wrist. "What do you mean?"

"Sit down, the two of you. Sit down," Kristy pleaded.

Mark felt a cannonball of tension come to rest in his stomach. "Let go of her, and everybody sit."

Erin pulled her wrist away from Jeremy and sat, glaring steadily and hatefully at him.

Jeremy sank slowly into his seat. "What do you mean?" he repeated slowly.

"I mean what I said. You heard me."

Jeremy closed his eyes for a moment, then shook his head slowly back and forth.

"You're lying. It's not possible. Lenny claimed the same thing that night."

Erin flared in defiance. "And so you killed him?"

Jeremy responded with a fiery glare of his own. "We were lovers eight, nine, and ten months before Raven was born. She has to be mine. You're lying."

"Lenny was my lover, too. You didn't know."

"Too? At the same time?"

Erin did not answer but stared stubbornly into Jeremy's eyes.

Mark decided he'd better try to exert some control over the situation, come what may from his interference.

"What she means is that the paternity of the child is in question."

Jeremy ignored Mark and glared at Erin, who glared back at him. "Are you telling me that you were screwing both of us at the same time? Raven could be the child of either one of us? Or is this another of your lies and trumped-up little games?"

Erin's bottom lip shook for a moment.

Kristy put her hand atop Erin's. "You must find out who the child's father is, Erin," she said softly.

"You damn well better find out," said Jeremy. "I goddamn demand you find out. Immediately!"

Erin began to cry and covered her face with her hands.

"Crocodile tears," Jeremy muttered.

Erin exploded. "I'll kill myself if you're the father. I'll kill myself. I don't want you near my child. You're evil, a murderer."

"Me? What you tried to pull on me in Pleasantville is worse than anything I've ever done. I'm not going away, sweetheart. I want to see my daughter."

"She's not your daughter!" Erin leaped to her feet.

Kristy rose and put her arms around the hysterical woman.

Mark rose and beckoned Jeremy. They moved a few feet away from the table. He held Jeremy by the arm and said, "It's likely true what she says about the two of you. You'd better believe it. She told us the same thing back in Pleasantville before all of this turmoil erupted. Look, they do tests now to decide this sort of thing. Finding out whether you're Raven's father won't be difficult. Leave Erin to Kristy. You can't accomplish anything today, not with this going on." He pointed to Erin still weeping in Kristy's arms.

"She's a pathological liar, my friend," Jeremy said, pulling his arm from Mark's grasp. "Don't believe anything she says or does." He paused a moment. "Yes, make her get the test. I want to know she's going to get the test. They'll need me, too. Here, take my cell number. I want to be sure she can contact me." He grabbed a paper napkin from a neighboring table and wrote his number. "Make sure she gets it. If I don't hear from someone asking me about this test in very short order, there's going to be hell to pay."

"Leave it to us," said Mark, willing to promise anything to get Erin and Jeremy apart for now. "I'll call you and let you know how things stand. Give it a couple of days. I won't leave you in the dark. I promise."

"Be sure." Jeremy spun and walked rapidly out of the restaurant.

Mark rejoined Kristy and Erin. "He's gone."

Erin's head came off of Kristy's shoulder. Mark took another napkin and handed it to Erin, who dabbed at her eyes with it.

A waiter approached with a gentle reminder. "Your food's been ready a while, folks."

"Bring it," said Mark. "Let's all sit down."

Most of the food went uneaten, as Kristy used the time to try and convince Erin of the necessity of determining Raven's father.

"It won't be him. It can't be," Erin said in desperation.

"Maybe it isn't," Kristy said softly.

"Let's get back to the theatre. It's time," said Mark.

~ * ~

Later, lying in bed, Kristy snuggled next to Mark and said, "What do you think Jeremy meant?"

"About what?"

"When he said Erin did something to him in Pleasantville."

Mark lay silent for a time.

"Hello, are you there?" Kristy whispered.

"I'm here. I don't know. Rejecting his request to see Raven and never contacting him, I suppose."

Now, Kristy lay in silence. "You think so?"

"I hope so. Did you get a chance to talk seriously to Erin?"

"We're having a drink tomorrow night. I think it might turn into something longer, though. Can you feed yourself dinner?"

"No, I'm totally dependent on you."

Kristy bit him lightly on the shoulder. Mark gave her a lingering kiss.

"Tomorrow, Miss King," he whispered into her ear, "since I won't have you for dinner, I intend on having you for breakfast. I'd like an eight-thirty reservation."

"There's no waitress service that early," Kristy whispered back. "You'll have to help yourself to whatever you want."

"Will do."

The conversation ended, and Mark let his mind drift pleasantly to the next morning and away from the events of the day gone by.

Thirteen

Kristy kept after Erin and finally, on the third day, Erin acknowledged she had no alternative but to determine the paternity of Raven. For the first two of those days, Mark kept his word and called Jeremy to tell him Kristy was trying, but Erin was resisting. With a profound sense of relief, Mark made the third call to Jeremy and announced Kristy's success.

"Tell her I expect to be contacted very quickly," Jeremy replied. Mark decided not to throw oil on a smoldering Erin and kept the message to himself.

Lady Windermere played to good audiences during the week, and the rehearsals for *The Winter's Tale* began.

Erin again asked to drop Raven at the theatre after the Sunday matinee to go off with Bob. Raven insisted on another trip to Columbus Park and another Chinese dinner—without bird beaks—and another movie—Mark chose *Pinocchio* this time—and Mark again had to undergo Kristy's gentle teasing about how good he was with Raven.

Kristy nestled up to Mark afterwards in the dark of their bedroom. "Wouldn't you like to be a father? You're not getting any younger, you know."

"Kristy, don't be ridiculous. I'm twenty-five."

"I think you're ready."

Mark knew Kristy meant she was ready.

"Sweetie, keep taking your pills and try not to surprise me."

Mark felt Kristy vanish for a moment. She rolled over, her back to him, and the conversation ended.

~ * ~

Rehearsals began again on Tuesday, and Erin made no mention of paternity tests. When the actors left for the day, Mark gave Kristy a questioning look. Kristy shook her head and shrugged. Neither of them had revisited the previous night's topic, and the chilly good night hadn't lingered into the new day.

The next day, Kristy took Erin to lunch. Late in the afternoon, as she and Mark walked home from the theatre, Kristy finally found an opportunity to report. They stopped in the Noho Star, a restaurant a few blocks from the theatre, and took stools at the bar.

"Update me," said Mark. "I need to know where Erin is on all of this so I can keep Jeremy cool and calm. He told me yesterday he hadn't heard from anyone yet about the test."

"Erin admitted she's in no hurry to go through with this, but she's contacted some outfit...what did she call it? DNA Diagnostics Center."

"Clever title. Took them a while to come up with it, I'll bet."

"Anyway, she contacted them."

"Did she tell Jeremy about this yet? Will the place call him? What happens now?"

"Erin mostly chattered on and on about how unsuitable Jeremy would be as Raven's father, but she promised to put everything in the hands of the Center."

"Let me call Jeremy and make sure he knows. I'll only be a minute." Mark stepped outside, and a moment later he was back at the bar with Kristy.

"He said they called him today—the Center."

"So, Erin told the truth."

"For once."

Kristy gave him a look of impatience.

"So how long does everything take, I wonder."

"As Erin truthfully explained to me, all the three of them need to do is to give a cheek swab and wait a week to ten days."

"All three? Why all three? Why Erin?"

"You want to know the truth?"

"All right. All right. Stop. What did Erin tell you?"

"They need a sample from her to let them identify and eliminate her DNA from Raven's. What's left over is the father's."

"Makes sense, I guess, mathematically speaking. What if they say Jeremy's the father? Can Erin wiggle out of it? What's the guarantee they're right?"

"If he's not the father, they're able to guarantee it one hundred percent. They can't be as absolutely certain if he is the father, only ninety-nine point nine, nine, nine percent sure."

"Not much wiggle room there. When will all of this happen?"

"After Thanksgiving. Erin plans to use the holiday to delay things a while."

"We'll know in early December. Where's the lab?"

"Uptown in the eighties."

"So, by the time we've finished *Lady Windermere*, Raven will be gifted with a daddy or not."

"Oh, she'll have a daddy, all right—a live Jeremy or a long-gone Lenny."

"I can't wait to hear," Mark muttered grimly.

~ * ~

Lady Windermere ended its run on a December Sunday. Erin remained close-mouthed about the testing, other than assuring Kristy she'd had it done. On Sundays, Erin continued to drop Raven at the theatre after the play and go off with Bob. On this Sunday, however, the cast celebrated the closing in Phebe's with the actors from both *Windermere* and the upcoming *Winter's Tale* in attendance.

The party had been underway for an hour when Kristy pulled Mark away from the clatter of the celebration.

"I'm worried that Erin hasn't shown."

"When did you last talk to her?"

"Friday afternoon, after rehearsal. She said she'd be here."

Mark shrugged. "I guess something came up."

"Something like the results of the test?"

"Why don't you give her a call?"

"I guess I better." Kristy reached for her purse and stepped outside of the restaurant. Mark moved to the bar where he could watch Kristy through the window. She opened her phone but paused. Jeremy appeared through the window, said something to Kristy, then entered the restaurant.

Mark's stomach twitched. Jeremy scanned the party, found Mark, and walked toward him. Over Jeremy's shoulder, he saw Kristy come back into the restaurant and move off to the side where she could watch the two of them.

"I'm surprised to see you here," said Mark. "Testing come off according to schedule?"

"I'm Raven's father."

Mark muffled a sigh. The melodrama would continue. "Congratulations."

"I need to talk to you. Erin is not taking the news well. I've just come from seeing her."

"When did you hear?"

"Yesterday."

"Erin heard at the same time as you?"

"More or less."

"What can I do for you?"

"I need to tell you some things. Things you have to believe. Erin is capable of...she's...she's... Listen, there are things you don't know, maybe you need to know."

"You're dancing around whatever it is you want to tell me. One thing I know. Neither one of you thinks very highly of the other."

Jeremy let his eyes meet Mark's. "I need to talk with you."

"So you keep saying, but we're in the middle of a party here."

"I know. I know. How about tomorrow then? I'll come over your way. Coffee at the Starbucks on Broadway near you okay?"

"Is this necessary, involving me? I don't know if I want to…"

"It's necessary. Believe me. Do this for me."

Mark took a peek at Kristy and saw her gaze still on him. An appellant such as Jeremy would be difficult to deny. "We're rehearsing at eleven," Mark said.

"Early then. Nine o'clock okay?"

Mark answered with a brief, "Yes," and after a muttered thank you, Jeremy left the restaurant.

Kristy came over to Mark. "And?"

"He's Raven's father."

"He told me."

"He wants to talk to me tomorrow morning at Starbucks. Did you reach Erin?"

Kristy shook her head. "I thought I'd better wait until after you finished with him. I guess I should call and commiserate."

"Don't mention I'm meeting him tomorrow."

Kristy gave Mark a quizzical look. "Why?"

"I don't want you to tell her anything she might react to. These two people…they're liable to go flying off into rages and diatribes at the drop of a…"

"Of a paternity test?"

Mark grunted his agreement.

Kristy went back outside, and Mark waited until he saw her talking on her phone before he stepped to the bar for another glass of wine. His glass was half empty by the time Kristy reappeared at his shoulder.

"She's wild," Kristy reported softly. "She won't have 'that murderer' in their lives. Her words. She won't share her child with anyone. I let her go on until she calmed down a little. She's getting a lawyer."

"As will Jeremy, no doubt."

"She said she'll see us at rehearsal tomorrow."

"There's a happy thought."

"Getting ready for the play seems to be an island of tranquility for her."

"Let's hope this island of hers isn't in the path of a hurricane."

Fourteen

The next morning Mark found Jeremy waiting at a table in Starbucks behind a crumb-covered plate and a cup of coffee.

"Had your breakfast, eh? Give me a minute," Mark said, and he went to the counter to get his own coffee and cake.

"Best seven-dollar breakfast money can buy," he said when he sat down across from Jeremy. "So, good morning."

"Morning."

Mark took a bite of his cinnamon coffee cake. "You called this meeting. The floor's yours. Kristy's meeting me here at ten. I can give you till then."

Jeremy took a breath, reluctant to start.

Mark gave him a nudge. "What did Erin do to you in Pleasantville? You've mentioned more than once that she did something."

"Look, what happened back in college to Lenny...just happened. I didn't mean for it to happen. I didn't want it to happen. When Lenny claimed to be the father of Erin's child, I snapped. I didn't think. I didn't believe it. I thought he was trying to provoke me. Jesus, I don't know what I thought." Jeremy glanced down at his empty plate. "I have a temper, and I paid for it. The idea, back then, of Erin dumping me or cheating on me...she's quite an alluring woman, you know."

Mark bent his head slightly, acknowledging Jeremy's opinion.

"She's very...I don't want to say sexy. Sexy's too common a word and not nearly strong enough. She's very...sexed, if you grasp me."

"I think I do."

"She's exciting to be with. She takes over your imagination, your fantasies, your life, but to understand her you have to realize—for her, outside of Raven, there is no 'other,' there's only 'self.' She has no sense of...of shame or regret, no hesitancy about simply doing what she has to do to get what she wants. She'll lie." Jeremy moved one hand in a swirl. "She'll force reality into the way she wants it to be. She has the ability to do that." He glanced at Mark intently.

Mark had taken Kristy's advice and dismissed trying to understand what motivated Erin, but now he feared Jeremy was on the verge of telling him things that would make his forbearance impossible.

"I don't believe it was an accident that her husband and I showed up at the same restaurant the night you and she had dinner together," Jeremy said.

"Why?"

"She visited me earlier in the day and promised to meet me at six o'clock—in that very restaurant. She told me she might be late. Ha! She wanted to be sure I stuck around."

"She never mentioned to me or Kristy she saw you that morning, and that she promised to meet you that night? Why didn't you mention this before?" Mark asked.

Jeremy gave a derisive snort.

"She'd only have denied it, but I figured out pretty quickly what she planned. Don't think her husband ending up at the wrong restaurant was an accident. I guarantee you, he went where Erin told him to go, at the time she told him to go there. She planned for us to bump into one another. She wanted us to be seen together. She hoped we'd cause a fuss. She counted on it."

"And you did cause a fuss."

"Not much of a one. Her husband came over and demanded I stay away from his family. Said the lawyers would handle things. My temper got the best of me, as it often does—I didn't like him using the term 'my family' against me—and we both shouted a little."

"You both left the restaurant about the same time. What time was it?"

"He got there maybe five minutes after me, so a little after six. After he showed up, I knew I wouldn't be meeting Erin there, so I left. He stayed on. I don't know when he left."

"Did you see him after you left the restaurant?"

"No. Why would I want to see him? He was a nobody, a nothing. He wasn't in my way. I didn't want his wife. I didn't want anything to do with his wife or with him. I simply wanted to see my daughter. When I left the restaurant, I went to Erin's house looking for her. The place was dark, though, so I didn't even get out of my car. I sat across from the house and waited a while, not very long. When another car pulled into the driveway, and I saw it wasn't Erin—it was obviously a man—I drove straight home. I figured it was Pete giving up on her, and I certainly didn't want to see him again."

"So you're saying...?"

"I'm saying, I hear you solve murders. Go to work and solve his because I assure you, I had nothing to do with it."

Mark put his coffee to his lips and sipped.

"Do you know a Bob Collins?"

"Bob Collins? No, why?"

"Just a thought."

"I visited Erin yesterday afternoon after I found out. She won't accept the news. Or me. So, I figured I'd try to find you. You appear to be reasonable and have some influence over her."

Mark ignored the complimentary mention of himself. "The courts will force her to accept your paternity. Whether your jail time factors in, I'm sure I can't say."

"She won't leave it to the courts. She'll do what I told you she can do. She'll twist and turn and orchestrate events and create the reality she wants."

"I don't see how she can do that. What reality are you talking about?"

Jeremy's voice grew agitated. "I'm talking about her making things work out so it's impossible for me to be involved in Raven's life."

Mark could feel Jeremy's leg bobbing nervously up and down beneath the small table.

Jeremy stared hard at Mark. "Look, I mean she'll do anything, and I mean anything, to have her own way."

"Are you suggesting she was somehow involved in what happened to her husband?"

Jeremy gave a quick, grim laugh. "I wouldn't put it past her."

"Come on. You don't really believe that."

"Somebody killed her husband, and I know it wasn't me."

"Erin was with us when it happened."

Jeremy shrugged. "You figure it out. It's what you do, isn't it?"

"No. I'm an actor."

"So is Erin, and how she manipulates the world to keep me away from my daughter will be her Academy Award performance, believe me."

Mark's interest had already veered away from Jeremy's story toward what he was going to do about Jeremy's story. He couldn't ignore it. If he did ignore the story, it would eat at him endlessly, and he'd had that kind of corrosive feeling before. To prevent a repeat of the feeling, he knew he'd have to take Kristy along with him every step of the way.

"Don't believe anything she tells you," Jeremy warned. "When she has tears in her eyes, she's laughing inside and vice versa."

"She can't lie about everything."

"You won't be able to tell when she's being truthful or not. I warn you."

"Me?"

"I'm warning myself, I guess, but you, too. She's a dangerous woman. I'm going to approach her with that understanding. So should you."

Mark nodded noncommittally, and both men rose.

"What do you do now?" Mark asked.

"I try to talk her into letting me see Raven, or I have my parents hire a lawyer and approach it through the courts."

"You sound pretty reasonable yourself. Are you living here in New York?"

"I found a tiny sublet down on Allen Street, a block below Houston."

"I wish you luck."

"Yeah, well, we'll see. Thanks for showing up."

Jeremy walked off down Broadway and Mark checked his watch. Five minutes later, Kristy came around the corner.

"I'm early."

"Did you come to peek in the window?"

"No. Did he show up?"

"He did. I'll tell you everything he said, and I'll tell you what we're going to do about it."

"You'll tell me what we're going to do about it?"

Mark smiled at her and winked. "Yep. Want to go to Brooklyn after rehearsal? Do you recall the name of the street where Bob Collins said he moved to? Dunham Place, wasn't it?"

"Yes, Dunham Place. Fifteen Dunham Place, if I remember. In Williamsburg."

"It's near our favorite restaurant."

"Giando's?"

"Yep. May I buy you dinner tonight?"

"You may." Kristy smiled, softening.

Mark took her hand, and as they walked uptown, repeated everything Jeremy told him. When he explained why he wanted to go to Brooklyn, she looked at him with concern, then took a deep breath and leaned her head against Mark's shoulder. When their eyes met, Mark knew Kristy finally realized his prying into Erin's life had become necessary.

Fifteen

"Ready to go in?" Mark asked. He and Kristy stood across the street from a small real estate office on Kent Avenue in Williamsburg, the closest real estate office to 15 Dunham Placc thcy could find.

"I suppose. You do the talking."

"You're an actress. Now act." Mark took her hand. They crossed the street and entered the office. A young woman sat at a small desk near the door, and a young man dressed in a business suit, his jacket hung on the back of his chair, studied some papers at another desk behind a low, wooden room divider.

Mark approached the woman after closing the door behind him. "Hi. A friend told me you have a loft available, and I'd like to get some information."

The man at the rear desk popped up to greet them. "Step in." He held open the swinging gate in the room divider. Mark and Kristy stepped through, and the man positioned two chairs before his desk.

"Sit, please." He gave them a big smile. "My name is George. Now, what was it you're looking for?"

"You have a loft at Fifteen Dunham Place, I believe. Around the corner," Mark explained. "A friend let me know about it. We might be interested."

"Dunham Place. Fifteen Dunham Place," the man mumbled as he typed the information into his computer. "Oh, I'm sorry. We rented the loft at Fifteen Dunham Place to an artist. We have a lot of artists coming into Williamsburg nowadays. Perhaps I can find something similar for you. Are you artists, too?"

"In a manner of speaking. Are you certain it's rented?" Mark gave Kristy a quizzical look. "How could Mandy get it so wrong?"

She shrugged. "Hard to believe, but you know Mandy."

"We heard only the other day it was still available. How long's it been off the market?"

"Let's see. The new tenant moved in…" George checked his big book. "October fifteenth. I'm sorry. Your information's a little out of date." George gave them an understanding smile. "It happens all the time. Good housing is a precious commodity here in New York, and the Dunham Place loft is a great work and living space for an artist."

"Well, I'm disappointed; aren't you, honey?"

"Crushed," Kristy responded.

"Okay, we'll keep looking. Thanks, George."

"I have a number of other places I could show you." George spun his computer screen toward Mark.

"Not right now, but I'm sure we'll be back. You have a card, George?"

George handed Mark a business card, and he and Kristy left the office.

Giando's, two blocks away along the river, overlooked the New York harbor and Lower Manhattan.

As they walked, Kristy said, "So you've answered your own question about when Bob decided to move to New York. He said at the opening he'd newly arrived."

"Yep. But now we know he arrived around the same time as Erin—a few weeks after the death of Pete. Looks like a whole relocation conspiracy. Plus, if he moved in mid-October, he had to have rented the apartment a while before that. Why not move in at the beginning of the month? What was he waiting for?"

"You tell me."

Mark stayed silent.

"Then you don't think their coming here at the same time was a coincidence?"

"Kristy, come on. She doesn't want anyone to know she and Bob knew each other in Pleasantville. That was the reason for the big show she put on meeting him in the gallery in front of us. And the reason for his saying he was from nearby Galloway rather than from Pleasantville itself. True?"

"Maybe he lives in Galloway."

"And when Erin said she's from Pleasantville, he doesn't mention he works there? More subterfuge."

"Probably."

"Pfft. Probably. Would she take up with a guy who was moving to New York if she didn't know she'd be moving away too, and why would he take up with a woman in Pleasantville when he knew he was moving away?"

Kristy shrugged unhappily in silent defeat.

"We don't know how long this was planned," Mark continued, "because we don't know how long they knew one another."

"Mark, if they planned to come here together, it would mean Erin knew she'd be able to come."

"Ah, I'm glad you see it. Their coming to New York together wouldn't be possible while her husband was still her husband."

"She might have been planning to leave her husband and simply run off."

"I think she would have told you big news like that, don't you?"

"Mark, she did have something to tell me. I know she did. I told you she did."

"But when she finally brought up the topic to us both, she said she was not running around with anyone. I don't see Erin having a problem admitting to you she'd met another man unless, suddenly, she needed to keep him a deep dark secret."

"She did have something to tell me. I'm certain of that."

"Yeah, well, why didn't she tell it? Look, it's a little before five. Let's plant ourselves at the bar in Giando's and nurse a glass or two of wine before dinner. We'll go over all the details of our visit to Erin and to Pleasantville."

"I can't believe this is necessary. I can't."

"But you agree with me. It is, isn't it?"

"Don't gloat."

They walked through the parking lot and up the six steps to the restaurant. The bar was lined with ten high-backed, upholstered chairs, eight of them empty. Mark led Kristy to the last two on the left. Outside the tall windows rose the towers of Lower Manhattan, and across the water, the South Street Seaport. The bartender hadn't come on duty yet, so one of the waiters appeared, poured two glasses of white wine, then vanished as quickly as he came. To their right past the bar, only two restaurant tables were in use.

Mark raised his glass. "To our collective memories. I hope yours is good."

Kristy gave Mark's glass a reluctant clink, and Mark began. "We agree, don't we, Erin and Bob knew each other in Pleasantville, and he had to be the guy she visited at the building, where we now know he worked. She did it a couple times when we were there."

"Hard to argue against. If we only knew how long they knew one another...one thing has always nagged at me."

"Speak right up."

"You know Erin said she found me through the newspaper article about the theatre."

"Yes."

"The article was six or seven months old. Where'd she get it so long after the fact?"

"Or she found it when it was current and held onto the information for six months. The question then would be, why did she save it for so long?"

Kristy faced the windows and stared at the glowing sun setting behind the skyscrapers of the city. "Mark, *Downtown Express* must have a website."

"Ah, technology. Of course, they have an online edition. I remember the reporter who wrote the article telling me I could find it online, but I didn't bother. I simply read it in the paper and never bothered with it on the computer. So, let's assume she googled you and found the article."

"Yes, she could have done that six months after the article appeared."

"She could have, but there must have been some reason you were on her mind at that particular moment. Let's hold off on that angle for now. What about your thinking she had something to tell you—something personal—in the kitchen summit meeting you mentioned?"

"I don't think it. She said as much," Kristy insisted. "She was leading up to something, talking about being disappointed with her life and feeling claustrophobic. Even the look in her eye..." Kristy trailed off.

"But she stopped and said she'd tell you later?"

"She said, 'Maybe later.' It must have been something about Bob. Had to be."

"It would make sense if she planned to tell you she was leaving Pete and moving to New York with Bob. It would explain Bob's finding an apartment when he did. They'd need a place to live when she made the move. But then came Jeremy."

"Yes! Jeremy's appearance could easily have complicated things and put this New York move out of her mind, so she never got around to telling me."

Mark spoke slowly, hoping Kristy would, again, fathom the implication of what she'd said without his having to spell it out. "Or Jeremy's appearance so affected what she wanted to tell you that telling you was no longer an option."

"Come again?"

"Jeremy showed up and complicated Erin's problem. Simply leaving her husband would no longer get her free. Jeremy would have been an even greater weight around her neck than Pete. She could dump Pete, but because of Raven, she couldn't dump Jeremy. Now, suppose Bob became part of a scheme Erin conjured up on the spot, and the scheme required they have no apparent knowledge of one another until they met in New York City."

"What scheme?"

"Come on," Mark chided. "Figure it out. Don't be so coy."

"So... you're suggesting she took advantage of the new situation with Jeremy to somehow remove her husband from the picture, and it involved Bob Collins? How?"

"Somehow remove her husband? You put it so delicately."

"She was leaving Pete anyway. She didn't need him dead."

"Jeremy showed up. I told you. Listen to me. After he showed up, simply leaving her husband would not make the world a simpler and better place, would it? Having Jeremy around would be as bad as having Pete around—worse because of his connection with Raven. Stop making me repeat myself. I'm sure the moment Jeremy showed up, Erin started conniving to get him out of her life, too. Now there were two men she wanted to disappear."

"You don't really think she had Bob...why didn't she have him kill Jeremy, too, since you're in such a bloodthirsty mood? Or kill only Jeremy, and return to her original plan and simply take Raven and leave for New York?"

"Jeremy is clearly a different animal. Maybe she couldn't control his whereabouts like she could control Pete's. Maybe she thought Jeremy would be too much for Bob—someone Bob couldn't possibly handle. Plus, a double murder might be a little too notorious even for Erin, don't you think? But she did come up with an idea of how to take care of two birds with one stone. Or in this case two stones. Two garden stones. She would frame Jeremy for killing her husband. If she got everyone at the right place at the right time, and the plan succeeded—which it did—both Jeremy and her husband would be out of her life. One dead, one put away for a long, long time. And let's not forget the collateral benefit: all the money she'd get out of Pete's death. Simply leaving him wouldn't have accomplished that."

Kristy nodded uncertainly. "You think she could talk Bob into... doing that?"

"Jeremy claims Erin can bend fate to her will. Bob strike you as a fellow who could say no to Erin? We know she stage managed the two of them to DiVito's at the same time so they would be seen together and perhaps interact, shall we say, in public. It happened."

"How'd she get her husband there?"

"Easy. She told him to go to the wrong restaurant on purpose. She found two restaurants with names similar enough to make it look like Pete made a mistake."

"But she called Pete from the restaurant when he didn't show up."

"Maybe she called his office because she knew he'd already left. Maybe she called where she knew he wouldn't be. She said he didn't answer his cell. Dubious, especially if he's somewhere waiting for her. Maybe she did call his cell because she knew he was dead already and couldn't answer. Remember what Jeremy said? Erin stopped off to see him that morning and promised to meet him at DiVito's in the evening, a meeting she obviously never planned to keep since she was going to dine with us someplace else."

"Maybe Jeremy's lying. He didn't tell this to the police even though it might have gotten him out of trouble."

"He said he didn't tell the police because he knew Erin would deny it. He couldn't prove they had a conversation. Erin never mentioned to us she had met Jeremy that day because she needed to keep it a secret. It didn't take Jeremy long to figure out what she was up to, and he decided to deal with her in his own way. Don't you remember him saying so when they had their little dust-up in Phebe's? Anyhow, we three went to dinner and Pete's late. Erin couldn't reach him. He couldn't call her because, fortuitously, her phone wasn't working."

In a soft voice, Kristy said, "Maybe you're right. He could have been dead by then."

Mark fiddled with his wine glass as Kristy waited to hear more. "Well?" she prodded. "Don't stop there."

"Suppose she was going to level with you and tell you about a lover, Mr. Bob, and she was leaving Pete and running off to Dunham Place. Jeremy shows up and everything gets extremely muddled. It explains the elaborate charade of meeting Bob at the art opening and doing it in front of witnesses. Us. They absolutely needed to be strangers to one another. No one would have seen them together back in Pleasantville, since their affair naturally took place behind closed doors."

"So, your conclusion is that Erin somehow had Bob kill Pete."

"It gets rid of the husband and provides her with a ton of money, gets her and her lover to New York and able to meet publicly, seemingly for the first time, with you and me as witnesses. She manages to point the crime toward Jeremy, even if only for the moment. It fits all the facts we know, doesn't it?" Mark added softly, "You said Erin was very lucky to have Raven. I'm not so sure the opposite is true."

They quietly sipped their wine and stared at the grand view across the river.

Finally, Kristy put her glass down on the bar. "Mark, I don't think..."

"Stop. I know what you're going to say."

"I'm going to say it anyway. You've strung an awful lot of maybes together. There's no real proof."

"Okay. How about all of the stuff about *The Winter's Tale*?"

"What stuff?" Kristy said impatiently.

"Greeting us with a quote from it...her college acting copy of the text happening to be in our bedroom, her harping on your acting, and her great desire to get back to acting. Let's go back to her tracking you down and inviting us at a time when she was, we believe," he raised a cautionary finger before Kristy could object, "contemplating a move to New York. Suppose one reason for her invitation to us originally was for her to wangle an acting job with AWB once she pulled off her imminent move to New York. I told you what Jeremy said to me—Erin bends events to her will; she shapes her own reality."

"That's not proof or evidence. It's only another maybe."

"Yeah, yeah."

Kristy put her hand on Mark's. "I know you think six maybes equal a probably, and two probablies equal a certainty, but there is no definite, hard fact in all of this, reasonably proving the events you've described happened in the manner and for the reasons you've postulated."

Mark faced her and acted astonished. "How the hell did you come up with a sentence like that?"

"How long have I known you? I've had about a year to practice, haven't I?' Kristy said sarcastically.

Mark gave a quick laugh and said, "I guess. So, you want an indisputable fact?"

"If you please."

"Okay. I'm indisputably hungry. Let's eat, but if I'm overly quiet during dinner, it will be because I'm looking for a second indisputable fact—one satisfying all of your criteria for certainty."

"I'll forgive you if you're quiet. I might even prefer it."

But over dinner, they rehashed their previous conversation, unable, however, to add anything of importance to it.

"What do you think we should do?" Kristy asked after their plates were cleared away, and Danny, the waiter, brought them two glasses of port. "Should we go to the police?"

Mark frowned at her. "No, no. We simply act as if everything's normal. As you so clearly put it, there is no unmistakable, hard evidence of anything. As I said, they were doubtlessly very careful back in Pleasantville or Galloway, wherever they had their trysts."

"Want to go see what Detective Moriarty thinks? He always looks forward to working on your little mysteries."

"A chat with Moriarty can't hurt, I guess."

Mark had met Detective Walter Moriarty of the New York City Police Department when a body, impaled by a sword taken from the properties closet in the theatre, had been found on the stage of the Bouwerie Lane Theatre. He and the detective had become friends and worked together twice afterwards when murder again invaded the world of the AWB cadre of actors.

"So how are we going to deal with your friend?"

"I told you to stop calling her my friend," said Kristy, her voice rising.

Mark could see Kristy was shaken by the possibility of Erin—her friend, despite her protests—being involved in a murder. He made a mental note that sensitivity and restraint might be the emotions of the moment in dealing with his lover.

"Suppose we do find the hard piece of evidence to show Erin was involved in all of this?"

Kristy took a shallow breath and said, "Then Erin will have a lot to answer for."

Sixteen

Mark met Detective Moriarty at a table in Phebe's at noon. The detective was short, overweight, and fiftyish, with an unmanageable mop of gray hair.

"Long time no see," said Moriarty, half rising from his chair to shake hands. He sat back down and patted himself on the stomach. "Put on fifteen pounds since my wife ran off." His wife had left him a few months back for an artist who lived up the Hudson River in Cold Spring, New York. "She's still up there cavorting around, but I told you all of this the last time we worked together. You got something good for me, I hope?"

"Maybe. How've you been otherwise?"

Moriarty shrugged. "Can't complain. I got my work, even though it's the same thing over and over, day in, day out. That's why I hope you got something good. You usually do. Kristy good? I know you had a rough patch."

"She's…we're…very well, but she has a friend I need to tell you about. Kristy knows I'm meeting you and telling you everything, and I'll go home and tell her everything we talk about. I don't want it to be like last time."

"She did get her nose out of joint over her brother, didn't she? So, start talking. Take your time. I don't gotta be at work till four, and I hate sitting home."

Over sandwiches, Mark told him everything he could remember. Moriarty interjected a question or two, but for the most part he simply listened.

"That's how it is," Mark concluded. "What do you think?"

Moriarty wiped his mouth with a paper napkin and shrugged. "Possible, the way you lay it out. The Pleasantville cops don't know nothing about this Bob Collins then?"

"I don't see how."

"Maybe somebody should give them a call and put them onto the guy. Tell them he needs some looking into."

"You mean me? Right. All I need is for Erin to know I think she killed her husband. Plus, why would the Pleasantville cops believe me?"

"Mmmm, no, no. I could call. I got credibility."

"What'll you tell them?"

"How about I say an anonymous tip came in on a case they're working on, a tip given to a credible New York City police officer? Me."

"I like the anonymous part. At least until I have something definite."

"There a number you can give me?"

Mark shook his head. "I have a name, though. Lieutenant O'Malley. He's the man who interviewed us after the murder."

"Lieutenant, eh? Usually pains in the ass. I'll get the number. No problem."

"Are you certain they'll follow up? They're a tiny police force."

"Ain't I credible? They'll follow up."

Mark stifled a chuckle. "Credible" seemed to be Moriarty's new word for the day.

"Okay, okay, you're credible. Will you call me?"

"Yeah. You moved...I know. Same number?"

"Same cell. Different landline. You have a pen?"

"Yeah." Moriarty shuffled inside his jacket, pulled out a small pad, and held it in front of him. "Like Columbo. Wait a minute." He wrote. "Pleasantville. O'Malley. And your number?"

Mark gave him the phone number and said, "Get this done for me, Detective, and you'll be more than credible. You'll be incredible."

Moriarty smiled and launched a thumbs up. "Ha! Yeah, I like that." Their conversation wandered to other subjects, and half-an-hour later they parted.

Later that night, Moriarty phoned and told Mark he'd made the call to Pleasantville.

~ * ~

Two days after conferring with Marty Schonbaum, Mark set the opening of *The Winter's Tale* for the second Thursday in January. The actors would remain hard at work in rehearsals, except for a few days off during the holidays. The current day's rehearsal would begin in thirty minutes.

When Erin showed up in the lady's dressing room, she said, "Kristy, I'm glad you're here."

"Hi, everything all right?"

"I don't know. I got a call from the police back home. They want me to drive down and talk to them."

"Really? About what? Did they say?" Kristy tried to gauge from Erin's manner whether she suspected Mark and her of having anything to do with the invitation. At the moment, though, Erin clearly seemed surprised.

"No, some 'new area of investigation,' they termed it."

"What in the world's that mean?" Kristy felt uncomfortable with this conversation. Working behind Erin's back was not an act she took lightly.

"Search me. Have coffee with me after rehearsal? You and Mark both? I don't get this at all."

"Sure."

When time and a cover of casualness permitted, Kristy found Mark in the tiny front office of the theatre.

"Erin wants to have coffee with us after rehearsal. It seems Moriarty is as credible as he claimed."

"The Pleasantville police contacted her?"

"They want her to drive down for an interview. She seems really flustered by it."

"Why do you think she wants to talk to us? Does she think we set her up?"

Kristy drew a deep sigh. "No, I don't think so, but I still don't want to think about it. Prepare yourself for anything, though."

"Okay, I will. Let's have everybody onstage and get started."

~ * ~

Four hours later, Kristy, Erin, and Mark sat at a table in a quiet corner of Phebe's.

"The play's coming along well, don't you think?" Mark offered in an effort to dispel the initial awkwardness of the meeting.

Erin offered an agreeable smile. "I'm having a blast, and I'm so grateful to you both." She concentrated on Mark. "Did Kristy tell you the police back home want to talk to me?"

"She did. Could they want more information from you about Jeremy?"

Erin shrugged. "Maybe. I can't understand how he managed to get off the hook."

"Maybe he really wasn't involved," Mark offered in a soft voice.

Erin shook her head. "No, he was. There's no other possibility. His temper, the situation, a thing he's done before..."

Mark chose not to argue the point. Instead, he asked, "When are you going?"

"They asked me to come tomorrow, but I told them we have rehearsal. They insisted, though. At least they offered to schedule it for six o'clock. I can still do rehearsal and make it. We're all in costume tomorrow, right?

"We are."

"I'll have to rent a car," she murmured.

"What about Raven?" Mark asked. "We'll take her for the afternoon and evening, if you'd like. She can even stay over if she wants." Mark could feel Kristy's eyes on him—an 'I-knew-it-all-along' stare. He ignored it.

"I didn't want to ask you. You've already done so much for me."

Mark waved off her reluctance. "No problem."

"Thanks, Mark. Okay if the babysitter brings her to the theatre after school?"

"That'll be fine."

"I'll cancel Bob this Sunday, so you don't need to do double duty this week."

"You don't have to," Mark assured her. "If Raven can stand us, we're happy to take care of her. Really. She's great company."

"She's a pleasure," Kristy added. Mark felt Kristy give his thigh a squeeze.

"You both do too much for me. You know, Mark, Raven's taken quite a shine to you. It's 'Uncle Mark said this,' and 'Uncle Mark said that.'"

"Uncle?" Mark said in surprise.

"She kept calling you Mark. I told her it should be Uncle Mark and Aunt Kristy."

"There's no need for that. Makes me feel antiquated," Mark said.

"I'm already the mother of a five-year-old," Erin said with a laugh. "How old do you think that makes me feel?"

"Any news about Jeremy?" Kristy asked.

"Not yet." A change came over Erin's manner like the drop of an icy curtain. "I wish he'd disappear. He keeps calling and asking to see Raven. He's not going to see her until I've done everything possible to prevent it."

Neither Mark nor Kristy responded.

"Anyway, I'll tell Raven *Uncle* Mark will be taking care of her tomorrow and Sunday afternoon. I don't think there's any need for her to stay over, but thanks." Erin rose, hugged Kristy, and thanked Mark again.

When she and Mark were alone, Kristy spoke. "What do you think she'll say when they ask her about whether she knew Bob back there?"

"She'll have to deny it. If she admits to it, she opens up far too many damaging possibilities, but she's going to wonder where they found Bob's name."

"Too late to worry about it now. Let's stop at the supermarket, and I'll cook tonight. Cooking and cuddling. Acceptable menu?"

"Sounds good to me."

"Great, Uncle Mark."

"Uncle Mark this." Mark tapped Kristy's arm lightly with his fist. "Let's go, and I don't want to hear one word about how good I am with Raven. I want to hear how good I am with you."

"Yes, Uncle Mark." Kristy rose, and smiling over her shoulder, sashayed toward the door.

Seventeen

Leontes: How blest am I
In my just censure, in my true opinion!
Alack, for lesser knowledge! How accurs'd
In being so blest! There may be in the cup
A spider steep'd, and one may drink, depart,
And yet partake no venom, for his knowledge
Is not infected; but if one present
The abhorr'd ingredient to his eye, make known
How he hath drunk, he cracks his gorge, his sides,
With violent hefts. I have drunk, and seen the spider.

The actors were working their way through *The Winter's Tale* in costume for the first time.

Hermione: Since what I am to say must be but that
Which contradicts my accusation, and

The testimony on my part no other
But what comes from myself, it shall scarce boot me
To say "Not guilty:' mine integrity
Being accounted falsehood, shall, as I express it,
Be so received. But thus: if powers divine
Behold our human actions, as they do,
I doubt not then but innocence shall make
False accusation blush, and tyranny
Tremble at patience.

Aside from a few stumbles here and there, both Marty Schonbaum, who would be given director's credit, and Mark were pleased and eager to continue to polish the performance. Raven showed up as Act IV ended and sat quietly in the back of the darkened theatre watching the actors on stage.

When the lights came on, she ran down the center aisle to Mark as the other actors left the stage for the basement dressing rooms. Mark made the two-foot jump down from the stage and greeted Raven.

"Well, how are you? Was school interesting today?"

"Do I have to call you 'Uncle Mark?' Mommy says I do."

"What do you think?"

"I think no."

"You don't want your Mommy to get mad, do you?"

Raven gave Mark a look of disappointment.

Mark felt a compromise to be in order. "Okay, look, let's make a plan. Mommy doesn't want you to call me Mark, and you don't want to call me Uncle Mark. So why don't we call each other Charlie?"

Raven laughed. "You're not Charlie. What were those people saying?"

"The actors?"

Raven pointed to the empty stage. "Those people."

"They spoke Shakespeare, a very special language. One day you'll think it's really beautiful and wonderful."

"I don't know what they're talking about."

Mark gave a laugh. "Don't worry. One day you will. Oh, here comes Mommy now. Ready, Charlie?"

Erin picked up her giggling daughter and hugged her. "What's so funny?" she asked and put her down.

Mark rolled his eyes up and acted innocent. "You'll have to ask my friend Charlie."

"Who?" Erin asked as Raven laughed again. Erin shook her head. "You two are goofy. It's three-thirty already. I have to go pick up the car. Be good, Raven. Give me another hug." Erin bid everyone farewell and headed off to Pleasantville.

The day was cold, but not cold enough to forego a trip to Columbus Park for an hour. Kristy cooked dinner at home—spaghetti with pepperoni and garlic bread.

Apropos of nothing, and after she'd swallowed a mouthful of spaghetti, Raven said, "I don't like Uncle Bob."

Kristy and Mark exchanged looks.

"Who is Uncle Bob?" Mark asked.

"He comes to visit a lot. Why do I have to call everybody 'uncle?' He wanted to babysit me, but I said no. I wanted you."

"Well, we're honored," said Mark, uncertain how far to take the conversation.

After a bite of bread and a glance at Mark, Raven said, "He didn't want Mommy to go today, but she said she had to."

"Oh, really?" Mark responded, feeling as if he were lifting a curtain better left hanging, but behind which might be a pot of gold available for the taking.

"Mark," Kristy cautioned.

He gave Kristy a glance.

"Where did Mommy go?" Raven asked.

"Didn't she tell you?" Kristy asked when Mark let the question go.

"Back home. The home where we came from. But how come?"

"Maybe she forgot something," Kristy suggested.

Raven shrugged and twirled her spaghetti clumsily around her fork.

An hour later, as Mark read to Raven, the phone rang. Kristy picked it up, and a few moments later joined Mark in the living room.

"Raven, Mommy called. She wants to know whether you'd be okay spending the night here and having Mark—Uncle Mark—take you to school tomorrow."

"In a taxicab?" Raven asked in an eager voice.

"You bet in a taxicab," Mark answered, quickly realizing it meant heading out into a chilly New York morning two hours earlier that his system was used to.

"I like taxicabs."

"Good. I told your mom you'd say yes."

"Read more. This one," said Raven, thrusting toward Mark one of the three vintage Golden Books Kristy had picked up earlier that day at the Strand bookstore and wrapped as a present.

"I read this one already."

"I like it."

"She likes it," Kristy added definitively.

"How many times do the kittens have to find their mittens?"

"As many times as they lose them," Kristy counseled. "Twenty more minutes, and it's time for your bath."

"I don't wanna take a bath," Mark moaned.

"Not you, silly."

Raven giggled. "Me! I like baths!"

"See, baths are good things," Kristy scolded. "And after yours, Raven, Uncle Mark will read you one last story before you go to bed."

Mark began to read, but Raven pushed down the book with her arm.

"Where do I sleep?"

"Don't look so worried. The sofa opens up," Kristy explained with a smile. "The one you're sitting on."

Raven studied the long living room and peered into the dark recesses of the dining area.

"It's adventure sleeping," Mark suggested, but a doubtful look swept over Raven's face nonetheless.

Raven glanced from the sofa to him, and the continuing look of doubt on her face sent a stab of guilt through Mark, though what exactly he felt guilty about befuddled him.

"I have an idea," he said. "Why don't you and Kristy sleep together in the big bed in the bedroom, and I'll be the lucky one to have the adventure sleeping." He crinkled his nose at Raven.

Raven smiled in relief and pulled the book out of Mark's lap.

"Read."

"Read. Yes. Get the bath ready," said Mark.

"Read," Raven insisted.

"Read," Kristy echoed and walked away laughing.

"I'm reading; I'm reading. Here kitty, kitty, kitty."

After her bath, Raven fell asleep midway through Mark's second additional reading of how the kittens lost and found their mittens. Mark gently nestled the covers around her and then returned to the living room. Kristy sat on the sofa, a glass of red wine in her hand, and a second full glass on the coffee table awaiting Mark. Kristy patted the sofa cushion next to her.

Mark fell wearily beside her. "So, this is what it's like, eh? I'm going to surgically attach those freakin' mittens to the paws of those freakin' kittens," he sing-songed. "Let them try to lose them then. Or I'll send them to freakin' Plantation, Florida, where they won't need any freakin' mittens." He reached for the wine and took a long sip.

Kristy laughed and smacked his thigh. "You love it, and don't say you don't." They saw in each other's eyes a glimpse of something that looked like the future. Neither commented on it, and Kristy said, "But more to the point. Bob...?"

"Yes, what do you make of Bob not wanting Erin to go to Pleasantville? I doubt it's because he'll miss her so much when she's away. If he's worried about what they might ask Erin, then he's worried something she might say would do some harm to him—which we both believe is possible."

Kristy shook her head. "I guarantee you they will get nothing out of Erin that she doesn't want to give them."

"Bob, it seems, is not as certain of Erin as you are."

"You think he might be worried they'll want to talk to him?"

"Today will be the first time she hears his name come up in connection with her and her husband. Depends on how she handles the shock of hearing his name. If she's as cool a customer as you think, she'll manage to keep him out of the narrative."

Kristy sipped her wine. "So, what do we do next?"

"Nothing but wait for a report, I suppose." Mark sipped his wine.

"We'll see her tomorrow at the theatre," Kristy said, "but she'll only tell us what she wants us to know."

"Not Erin's report. Moriarty's. He'll find out what really happened."

"Oh, I forgot about him."

"Anything you want to do tonight?" Mark asked.

Kristy shook her head. "We can't go anywhere. Can't make much noise."

"I'm going to try to read for an hour or so." Mark yawned. "Maybe less. Entertaining Raven and chasing after careless kittens takes its toll on a man."

"I'll read some, too. Let me get us another glass of wine."

"Thank you, darling." Mark leaned over and kissed Kristy, who rose and disappeared into the kitchen.

Mark read very little, though, because his mind would not leave Pleasantville and everything that had happened since he'd met Erin. He finally gave up, opened the sofa, and bedded down.

~ * ~

Kristy dressed Raven the next morning as Mark grappled with his early rising and strove to get himself into gear. He glared at Kristy as she waved good-bye and stretched luxuriously for his benefit. "Don't wake me when you get back," she teased.

Raven leaned against Mark, only half awake, as the taxi made the ten-minute drive to her school in Battery Park City.

"We're here, sweetie," said Mark, jostling Raven. "Enjoy the ride?"

"I think I fell asleep."

"Come on. You have to wake up now. School time." Mark took her by the hand.

They found Erin standing outside of the schoolyard. Raven ran to her.

"Good morning, precious," Erin said as she and Raven hugged. "Thanks, Mark."

"Always a pleasure."

"Wait here a minute, will you? Say thank you to Uncle Mark, Raven."

"Thank you, Charlie."

"You're welcome, Charlie," Mark replied, and he waited for Erin to return from depositing Raven in the proper line.

"So, how'd it go?" Mark asked as they left the children behind.

"Weird. They kept asking about Bob. Why would they ask about Bob? How did they even know about Bob?" She gazed at Mark.

Mark felt her gaze but kept his face forward. "Search me." Mark seemed to ponder the question. "That is weird, isn't it?"

"It really is. Pleasantville's dinky police force certainly doesn't have its fingers into things up here in New York City."

"What did they ask you?"

"All about Bob," Erin repeated, her voice rising. "I told them I met him at the opening. I mentioned you and Kristy were there. They may call you about it. Sorry to drag you into it, but I didn't know what else to tell them."

"Don't worry about it. Honesty's always the best policy. I see a cab. I'll catch you later at the theatre."

"Bye, and thanks again."

Mark waved his arm at the approaching taxi. As the taxi swerved to a halt, he said, "Anytime. I'm looking forward to Sunday. Bring Raven over early. The earlier the better." Mark closed the taxi door and did not look back.

Eighteen

At one-thirty on Sunday, a week before Christmas and a few days after Erin's interview with the Pleasantville police, Mark's apartment buzzer proclaimed the arrival of Raven and Erin.

"Here she is," Erin announced as she and Raven came through the doorway.

"In a hurry? You seem rushed," said Mark.

"Bob's waiting downstairs. Be good, sweetheart." Erin kissed Raven and left.

"Let me help you with your coat," said Mark.

Raven gave a prodigious yawn.

"Aren't you a sleepyhead today!"

Raven shrugged, stood, and spun around as Mark dealt with her coat.

The Cartoon Channel played on the TV, and Raven fell onto the sofa in front of the screen. Kristy entered the apartment carrying two grocery bags.

"I passed Erin coming out of the building," she said.

Mark gestured toward Raven, whose eyes were closed. "She's very quiet today," Mark said to Kristy. "Are you feeling all right, Raven? Does your head hurt?"

Raven opened her eyes and shook her head.

"Why so sleepy today?" Mark prodded. "Were you out late at a party?"

Raven shook her head.

"Stay up late watching TV?"

Raven shook her head again.

"Bad dreams keep you awake?"

Raven shrugged.

"Bad dreams, eh? I have them sometimes, too."

"Mommy and Uncle Bob made a lot of noise. I couldn't sleep."

"Uncle Bob," Kristy murmured in mild distress.

"Maybe they had bad dreams, too."

Raven, her eyes on the TV screen, shook her head. "They were awake. Mommy said she was afraid he would break something, but he said he wouldn't." She shrugged.

Mark and Kristy exchanged looks. Kristy indicated he should leave the child alone. "Take one of these bags," she said and motioned him into the dining room. "Put it on the table, and I'll take care of it." She lowered her voice. "They must have kept the poor kid awake arguing about something. What do you think?"

"What could it be Bob would break? His silence? His promise?" Mark wondered grimly. "I wonder..." He went to the kitchen wall phone.

"Now what?" Kristy asked.

Mark punched in the number.

"Who...?"

Mark raised his hand to silence Kristy.

"Detective? Hi, Mark Louis here. Yeah, fine. You, too, I hope. Listen, I was wondering if you heard how Erin did with her interview the other day. Yeah, I saw her, and she's perplexed at how they knew about Bob. No, if she suspects Kristy and me, she didn't show it. I don't know. Kristy and I are babysitting the little girl, and she says Erin and Bob argued last night. I'm guessing Erin's nervous about Bob holding up under pressure. Can you find out whether Pleasantville has any plans to talk to him? If they don't, I think they should. Use some more of your incredible credibility and get him an invite. Guarantee them he's more likely to make a slip than she is." Mark eyed Raven, who seemed dead to the world. "Yeah, please. Thanks, I'll talk to you later." He hung up and faced Kristy. "He's going to talk to them."

The phone rang, and Kristy picked it up, listened a moment, and handed the phone to Mark. "It's Jeremy."

Mark puffed out his cheeks with a sigh, took the receiver, tapped himself on the ear with it, and pointed to the bedroom. Kristy hurried into the bedroom and picked up the extension. When she appeared at the bedroom door, the phone to her ear, Mark said hello.

Jeremy said, "I thought I'd call and see whether you had any news about Erin. About her letting me see Raven. I get nowhere with her. You two seem to have her ear."

"No, no news. As a matter of fact, Raven's asleep on my sofa at the moment."

"Your sofa? Why's that?"

"Kristy and I have been babysitting her on Sundays while Erin does some chores."

"Chores, right. You're very discreet. She's probably off with her photographer friend."

"You know about him?"

"Erin happily brings him up whenever I manage to talk to her. Listen, you think I can see Raven, since she's with you?"

Kristy shook her head.

"Jeremy, you're putting me into a spot. I don't have any authority to do that. Erin would probably go nuts, and she is a friend of ours."

"Mark, I simply want to look at her. She is my daughter, and her damn mother won't let me near her unless a court of law intervenes. You know that could take forever."

"No, I can't do it. Suppose Erin found out and used it against you when this court thing came up. You might be hurting yourself."

Mark's logic silenced Jeremy for a moment. Then he said, "Are you taking her out today?"

"I usually do."

"So, walk her by me. I won't talk to her. I only want to see her. Where do you take her?"

"Usually to a park down in Chinatown, and afterwards we get some Chinese food."

"Which park?"

"Columbus Park."

"Yeah, I know it. Let me watch her play. I swear I won't interfere. Come on, let me see her."

Mark drew in a deep breath as Kristy waggled her head indecisively.

"I don't know what time she'll wake up."

"You have my number. Call me when you leave the house. I'm not far from Chinatown. Mark, I swear I won't bother her or you."

Mark considered, sorry he'd mentioned Raven in the first place. "I can't promise. Raven's very sleepy today for some reason. If she's sick or getting sick, I won't be taking her out."

"I understand. But if you do take her out...?"

"All right. All right. I'll call you. But keep your word."

"Great. I will. I swear. Thanks. I'll be waiting. Bye."

Kristy disappeared for a moment to replace the phone.

"What do you think?" Mark asked a moment later when they sat at the dining table.

"I don't know. He sounds genuine, but we're doing an awful lot of things behind Erin's back."

"You think?"

"Yes, I think. Well, go relax until Raven wakes up. I have bills to pay." Kristy moved to the end of the long dining table and plucked the bills out of the chaos of papers thrown there.

Mark quietly gathered up the current book he was reading and sat in a chair in the living room, keeping one eye on Raven, who slept for another two hours.

"Well, look who's back." Mark said. He'd also fallen asleep in his chair for a short while. "Do you feel all right?"

Raven rubbed her eyes. "I think so."

"Not sick are you?"

Raven shook her head.

"What do you want to do?"

"Play."

Mark laughed.

"Play what? Play where?"

"In the park, like always. Will you take me?" Raven hopped from sofa and climbed into Mark's lap.

"It's pretty cold out there."

"And egg rolls, too."

Mark laughed. "And egg rolls, too? You want to try the ones with bird beaks this time?"

"No!"

"Okay, let's dress you up real warm." While Kristy bundled up Raven, Mark phoned Jeremy.

Thirty minutes later, Raven was running and climbing with a host of other children out on the brisk but sunny afternoon.

Jeremy was already seated on a bench holding a newspaper when they arrived. He acknowledged Mark and Kristy and folded up his paper. True to his word, he stayed on the bench and simply watched. After an hour, Mark and Kristy led Raven to Mott Street and their usual restaurant. Back home at six o'clock, they found Erin waiting at the front door of the building.

"Mommy," Raven cried and ran to her.

"You're very early today," Kristy said. "Want to come up? You have to come up. Raven has her bag of toys upstairs."

As they climbed the stairs to the apartment, Mark could sense that Erin was not her usual self.

"Let me get you something to drink while you warm up," Kristy offered. "Did you get your chores done?"

"Some," said Erin brusquely. "Bob left early."

Kristy handed her a glass of white wine.

"Something about a busy day tomorrow," Erin explained. "I did get some Christmas shopping done."

The talk moved to the theatre and the final rehearsals for *The Winter's Tale*. Erin drained her glass and set it down. "I see Raven's things." She walked to the long wooden dining table. She picked up Raven's bag and paused. A business card lay atop a mess of papers next to Kristy's checkbook. Erin picked it up and studied it.

"Thinking of moving, Kristy? And to Brooklyn?"

As Mark buttoned Raven's coat, both the question and Erin's icy tone caught his attention.

"Whatever gave you that idea? We only just moved in here," Kristy answered.

"Real estate agent." Erin held the card between two fingers and waved it before tossing it back onto the pile of papers.

Lacking a quick answer, Kristy shook her head and managed, "That must be from long ago."

"Raven's ready to roll," Mark called.

Good-byes circulated, Erin's lacking its usual warmth.

"See you tomorrow at the theatre," Mark said as he closed the apartment door.

Kristy stood near the dining room table studying the business card Erin had inspected.

"What is it?" Mark asked.

"It's the card from the real estate office in Williamsburg."

"Ouch. What's it doing there?"

"I took it out of your pants pocket when I did the laundry. I must have tossed it there."

"You think she connected it with Bob?"

Kristy made a 'wasn't that obvious?' sound. "She read the address, didn't she? She's no doubt suspicious already about how the Pleasantville police knew about Bob. Now, she finds we have a business card from the real estate office in the neighborhood where he found his apartment. She's liable to connect things. Why did I leave it there?" she moaned.

"I better remind Moriarty to follow through and get the police to interview Bob. I'll call him right now."

"You just talked to him. He's going to think you're a pest."

Mark phoned Moriarty, who assured him he'd make the call first thing next day.

Nineteen

Detective Moriarty did not call back until Monday evening. After they'd spoken, Mark hung up and waited impatiently to give Kristy a report. In a robe, barefoot, and with a towel wrapped around her wet hair, she emerged from the bathroom.

"Did I hear the phone? What's up?" She stood near the sofa.

"They're going to interview Bob. Moriarty has them believing he could be the weak link in Erin's scheme."

Kristy wasn't convinced. "All he has to do is say he didn't know Erin until they met in New York, and there goes any motive. He probably doesn't even need an alibi for the murder. He could say he sat home all night alone. It's months ago. Who could contradict him?"

Mark stared quietly at her.

"What?"

"I hate it when you're so logical, but you're right, I'm afraid. If both of them stick to claiming they met at the opening..." Mark shrugged. "There's no way to get at them. We'll need to find some way to show they knew each other back in Pleasantville to have any shot at this. I wish we could go back to when we saw Erin saying good-bye in the doorway. I'd run across the street and yank whoever it was out onto the sidewalk. It would be Bob, I guarantee you."

"Yeah well, I'm fairly certain time travel's out. We saw a hairy arm. Bob have a hairy arm?"

"Normal hairy for a man. He's not going to break down over his arm hair."

"When is his interview going to happen?"

"They planned to contact him today. If they reached him, then either tomorrow or Wednesday."

"How do you think Erin will react when she finds out?"

"What with keeping poor Raven awake arguing and cutting short their Sunday afternoon together, I don't think she has total confidence in Bob."

"All he needs to do is say he didn't know her then."

"I know. I know. So you've reminded me more than once. We need some hard piece of evidence to prove Erin and Bob knew one another before they came to New York City."

"So you've reminded me more than once. I'm dripping. Let me get dressed." Kristy headed back to the bathroom, and for the umpteenth time, Mark started at the beginning and traced his history with Erin.

~ * ~

The AWB troupe planned rehearsals on Tuesday and Wednesday before breaking for Christmas. They planned three days of brief scene rehearsals the next week before a final week of rehearsal after New Year's. They would open the second Thursday in January. Erin quietly attended to her business on Tuesday, not acknowledging Mark or Kristy other than to give them an obligatory greeting and farewell. Tuesday night, Moriarty called and reported to Mark. Kristy watched Mark during the conversation.

When Mark hung up, he gave Kristy a slight grin and said, "They interviewed Bob today, and he stuck to the party line, but they're asking both Erin and Bob to drive down again on Friday. Moriarty says Bob didn't impress the Pleasantville police as a reliable customer."

"Wow! You think they'll force Bob to fall apart?"

"I don't know, but he won't be any calmer for making the trip down with Erin drumming the need for obedience to her into his head."

"She didn't say much to either of us today."

"I noticed. She'll probably have even less to say tomorrow after she hears from Bob and gets her next invitation to Pleasantville."

Erin, it turned out, had quite a lot to say the next day. After the cast ran through the play, she approached Kristy.

"I'd like to talk to you and Mark."

"Sure," Kristy agreed.

"Alone. I'll wait over there until everyone's gone." Erin indicated a seat in the front row of the audience, and Kristy saw the challenge in her eyes. She hurried downstairs to find Mark.

"Erin wants to talk to both of us, but only after everyone's left. She's waiting upstairs."

"Uh-oh. She say what it's about? Give you any hint?"

Kristy shook her head. "Her cold eyes were hint enough."

"Oh, boy."

When the rehearsal ended, Mark and Kristy bade farewell to the other actors, wished them the cheer of the season, then made their way upstairs to Erin.

"Did you want to talk to us, Erin?" Mark asked in what he hoped was a neutral tone.

"I do. Did you know Bob travelled back to Pleasantville yesterday?"

Mark spread his hands, questioning the relevance of the question.

"They asked him questions for two hours."

"They who?"

Erin shook her head in disbelief.

"The police, Mark. Don't act like you didn't know."

"Questioned him about what?" Mark responded, ignoring whether he had known or not.

"About whether he and I knew one another when we lived back there. They asked where we met. They asked when we met. All things they'd asked when they questioned me." Her voice rose. "They asked what Bob was doing the night Jeremy murdered my husband."

"Why Bob?" Mark asked.

"Because someone is trying to convince them Bob...and I...had something to do with Pete's death. They want both of us back again on Friday. It's you, isn't it? Both of you."

"Both of us what?" Mark asked, refusing to release his gaze from Erin's.

Erin gave an angry sigh. "You both think I had something to do with Pete's death. You both think Bob had something to do with it, too. It's obvious from the questions the police asked. The questions all revolve around the time both of you were in Pleasantville, and Bob and I meeting at the gallery. It's obvious you've been talking to them, but why would you lie about me so? You never saw me with Bob in Pleasantville, because I was never with Bob in Pleasantville. I met him at the gallery opening. You were there."

Mark heard Erin's challenge and decided to meet her head on.

"No, you didn't meet him there, Erin. You staged the meeting at the gallery for Kristy's and my benefit." He felt Kristy move near him as the battle flamed into the open.

Slowly, Erin shook her head. "You're wrong. Bob and I were never together in Pleasantville. No one can say we were...well anyone can say it, but no one can prove it. Certainly not the two of you, hanging around for, what...all of two days?"

Anger crept over Mark. Erin's certainty that she'd planned things to perfection galled him. He couldn't let it stand. "You somehow sent your husband to the wrong restaurant. Earlier in the day, you told Jeremy you'd meet him at the same restaurant where you sent your husband. The two men bumped into one another and naturally were seen together. Later, someone killed your husband."

"Yes, Jeremy."

"Not Jeremy. Bob."

Erin gave a sarcastic laugh. "Impossible. He had no reason to. We didn't even know each other then."

"You and Bob have been arguing lately. What are you both worried about? Bob cracking? Bob not being able to hold up his end of things and stay quiet? He's not as strong as you, is he? You think he may not be able to get through another interview, don't you? The police must have found out something more about the two of you to invite you back again, and I don't think Bob will be able to handle the pressure."

"Raven," Erin muttered softly. "You've been pumping Raven for information about me, haven't you? Unbelievable! Well, that stops now. You've seen the last of Raven, and as for Bob, he's already gotten through one interview with the police, and he can get through as many as they'd like to have. He has no reason to worry. The truth is on his side—he and I never met until we met in front of the two of you."

"No, you're lying. You knew each other before because the two of you planned to move to New York at the same time."

Erin blithely spread her hands. "So? Of course, he moved to New York. How else could I bump into him unless he moved to New York? I don't see any sense at all in the point you're trying to make."

"The point is: you and Bob planned to come to New York together after you'd left Pete, but when Jeremy showed up on your doorstep, the whole plan needed to change. You wanted both men, Pete and Jeremy, out of your life." Mark felt the traction of his argument slipping away as he sensed the relaxation creeping into Erin's manner.

"Good luck trying to establish that. After Jeremy killed my husband, I had the opportunity to do what I always wanted, what Kristy was so lucky to have done. I came to New York. I have an acting job. I will get other acting jobs. I will be an actress. And I will raise my daughter in the manner I see fit."

Erin sent a challenging look from Mark to Kristy and back again. "I want you both to butt out of my life. You know nothing about me. You know nothing about Bob. You know nothing about us." Erin paused a moment. "I will see you next week for rehearsal. Happy holidays." She strode past Mark and Kristy, leaped the short distance to the stage, and disappeared into the wings.

"Well," said Kristy softly.

"She did it. She planned the whole thing."

"I believe you, but how do you prove it?"

"There has to be some way to show they knew each other before their nonsensical meeting at the gallery."

"Talk to Moriarty. He may have some ideas."

"Let's go home." With that, they both left the theatre.

Twenty

By the time Mark reached home, his anger at Erin's smug confidence had transformed into an impassioned promise to Kristy that he'd find a way to prove her guilt. "We know Bob is the link where the chain will have to break, if it's going to break at all."

Kristy slumped onto the sofa. "Metaphorically true, darling, but how?"

"I'll go see him. I'll tell him I'm certain of what he did. I'll tell Moriarty to suggest to the Pleasantville cops they lean on him hard and use every trick they ever heard of."

"If you go see Bob, I want you to take Moriarty along. Bob is a killer, you know."

"I will. They go for the interview on Friday, so I'll have to see him tomorrow. How, though?"

"You could try knocking on his door."

"I hope it's that simple, but what if he's not there? Suppose 'Uncle Bob' is at Erin's house. I don't see myself talking to him in front of

Erin. He probably will be at Erin's tomorrow night if they're traveling together the next day. Where's his photography studio?"

"I don't know. Want me to call Erin and ask?"

"Mmm, you do that." Mark thought back. "Kristy, the day in Pleasantville, we visited Bob's studio."

"I remember."

"We took a business card. What pants did I wear? You found the real estate agent's card when you went through my pockets. Did you find the card from Bob's studio when you did the laundry? You must have."

"It's almost two months ago. I don't remember. I must have, though. You know, you could empty your own pockets sometimes." She walked toward the dining room table, its near end littered, as always, with papers. "Whatever was in your pockets, I'd have tossed here, as usual." She dug through the pile. "What a bunch of junk... here...no. Who the hell is Dr. Alcott?" Kristy tossed aside a business card for a Dr. Alcott.

Mark bent to retrieve a handful of papers that had slid to the floor. He shuffled through them.

"Here," said Kristy. "Artistic Photography. I found it." She handed it to Mark, who took the card and walked into the kitchen. He punched in the number on the wall phone.

"What are you doing? He's not there, remember?"

"I know but..." He held up his hand and repeated what he heard. "The number has been changed. Get a pen, quick."

Kristy grabbed a pen, and Mark recited the number.

"Give me." Mark entered the new number and listened. A few seconds later, he punched in the number 2 and wrote down the new address of Artistic Photography.

"His studio's located at one sixty-three Broadway in Brooklyn. The recording said, right on the other side of the Williamsburg Bridge. Same neighborhood as Dunham Place."

"Makes sense. He works near where he lives. Giando's is right down the street, too."

"He'll probably be working tomorrow."

"Who are you calling now?"

"Moriarty...to see if he's free tomorrow."

~ * ~

The next afternoon, Mark met Detective Moriarty at Phebe's for lunch, and together they plotted out their approach to Bob. Moriarty drove to Brooklyn. The detective put a police placard in his car window and parked in what would otherwise be an illegal spot diagonally from Bob's studio.

Without speaking, Mark and Moriarty crossed the street. They waited until the only two customers in the store left. Moriarty took his place alongside the door ready to flash his shield and inform anyone interested in patronizing Artistic Photography the store would reopen in fifteen minutes.

"Good luck, pal," Moriarty said.

Mark took a deep breath and entered.

"Mark!" cried Bob.

"Can I lock the door?"

"What?"

"I'm locking the door." Mark flicked the latch.

"What's going on?"

"I'm here to tell you it's all over, and I know pretty much everything."

Bob's face clouded. "What are you talking about?"

"I'm talking about you and Erin being responsible for killing her husband. I know she got you to do it."

Bob stiffened and set his jaw defiantly.

"You're crazy. I didn't even know Erin until I came to New York."

"Oh, really? I think you did. You both planned this move to New York well before you met at the gallery. Since you lied about that, it suggests other lies. Erin planned to leave her husband and join you in New York, but then Jeremy showed up, and the complications over dealing with him—and dealing with Erin's desire to keep Raven to herself—changed everything. She arranged for both her husband and Jeremy to go to the restaurant where they met that night. Erin's husband couldn't contact her because her cell phone was dead, and he didn't know what else to do but go home, where you waited for him."

"I don't know what you're talking about. I never met Erin until I saw her in the gallery. You were there."

Mark smiled and shook his head. "Erin's convinced you that repeating your little mantra will save you, but it won't. Your meeting her in the gallery was as phony as a three-dollar bill. Erin said she picked up the postcard announcing the opening in her building. Her building doesn't allow distributions like that. You probably gave it to her—easy enough, since you'd obviously been in the gallery earlier to set up your part of the show. She wanted your meeting to have witnesses. Very heavy-handed, Bob."

"Maybe somebody dropped the card in the elevator, and she picked it up."

Mark shook his head. "There was no earthly reason for such a staged meeting between the two of you except to establish the fact you didn't know each other in Pleasantville, and you and I both know why that was necessary. You and she are having a rough patch right now, aren't you? What's the point of contention? Where's the rub? I think I know. She's worried about how well you'll lie to the police, isn't she? I think that's it. And you're probably worried about it, too."

"We're not having any kind of patch. We're fine. I met her at the gallery. You were there. I have no reason to lie about anything."

"You never told us your photo studio was on Main Street in Pleasantville. You led us to believe you were based in Galloway. Another lie, Bob. I found the building in Pleasantville where you worked. I saw Erin visit the building twice during the time I was there. She was visiting you, obviously. You said good-bye to her once at the front door of the building when she was on her way to meet me for lunch, and you even looked into her car when Kristy and I waited for her the first day of our visit. It took a while, but I recognize you now."

Confusion rose in Bob's eyes. Mark struck again. "The police know all of this, Bob, and tomorrow..."

"All you need to know—all they need to know is that I didn't meet Erin until we came to New York. It's no secret I had a studio in Pleasantville. Now, get your ass out of here before I call the police."

Mark unlocked the door. "Detective." Moriarty walked in. "Here's your policeman, Bob."

Moriarty took out his wallet and displayed his shield. Added confusion swept over Bob.

"Get him out of here then, Officer. He can't come in here and lock my door and threaten me. How dare you?"

"Come on, Mark," said Moriarty.

"Yeah, go," said an emboldened Bob. "You prove me a liar. Go on, try. I didn't know Erin until I met her right in front of you. End of story. Now, get the hell out of here."

Anger swept over Mark, but he felt Moriarty's hand on his arm and allowed Moriarty to move him toward the door.

"I will prove you a liar. You and Erin both," Mark promised Bob as he closed the shop door behind him.

Moriarty glanced at Mark as they crossed the street. "You trying to get me fired?"

"He's an arrogant bastard."

"No reason to get me fired."

"Yeah, I'm sorry. I couldn't help it."

They seated themselves in Moriarty's car.

"He's right, isn't he?" Moriarty asked.

"About...?"

"You needing to prove he knew the lady back in Pleasantville."

Mark sat quietly as Moriarty maneuvered the car onto Broadway for the trip back to Manhattan. Moriarty repeated himself. "Isn't he?"

"Yes, yes," Mark snapped. "Kristy tells me. You tell me, and I already know it, anyway. If he didn't know Erin in Pleasantville, why would he be involved in the murder of her husband? If he did know her, it proves he's lying, and their whole story crumbles."

"So, can you?"

"Prove they knew one another?"

"Yes, prove they knew one another."

"No. Not yet, anyway."

"They're being interviewed tomorrow at one o'clock. Doesn't give you much time. Why don't you talk to Pleasantville? Tell them everything you know and everything you suspect. Let them use it in their questioning tomorrow. You know more about what happened—what you think happened—than I do. They should hear from you, don't you think? Can't hurt. We get back to your apartment, I'll make the call, and you do the talking."

Mark began to compose what he would say.

Twenty-one

That night, Mark and Kristy sat in their living room discussing Erin.

"Her dead cell phone was too damned convenient."

Kristy shrugged. "Batteries die. Mine did last week. Can't be helped."

"But I'm such a dunce. It's so obvious to me now. Her phone had to be dead so Pete couldn't call her and check on the correct restaurant. He'd have no other choice but to go home after the restaurant asked him to leave and Erin didn't turn up."

They'd gone over their trip to Pleasantville three times, and in Mark's mind, Erin's dead cell phone had become the keystone to the evening.

"She tried to track him down," Kristy said. "She called his office, his cell, and their home."

"Are you sure?"

"She called right at the table on my phone."

"Where is your phone?"

Kristy pointed.

"Do you mind if I scroll through your old calls? Maybe she knew his schedule so well she knew where he *wouldn't* be at any particular moment. She knew he wouldn't be home. She knew he'd have left work by that time of night. She left us, if you recall, and ended up in the corner of the restaurant."

"To scold him out of earshot, we decided."

"She didn't scold him, though. She said he didn't answer his cell, but there's no way she called his cell...how could she? He'd have picked up, wondering where she was. She didn't want to get in touch with him and tell him where she was. She wanted him to go home. Where the hell are your calls from October?"

"I always delete calls from the previous month. It seems unnecessary and so cluttery to keep them around."

"Cluttery," Mark grumbled and tossed the phone onto a stack of papers lying on the dining table. "I wanted to check on those calls Erin made that night and see whether she really did call Pete's cell phone. Wireless bills used to show every call you made, but they don't anymore. They only tell you to send money."

"You can do that online, you know."

"Do what? Send money?"

"Send money, of course. I mean you can see the calls you made over any billing period."

"Really? I didn't know that. Do it for me. Please?"

She smiled. "Mr. Helpless. Watch and learn."

A few minutes later, Mark, looking over Kristy's shoulder, tapped her. "I'll take it from here." Kristy left the computer, and Mark took her place. Speaking mostly to himself, he said, "The October dates would be on your most recent bill. October," he muttered and tapped the computer keyboard. He scrolled to the proper date. "Ha! Technology is great when it works. Here's the day we want. I see...holy shit!"

"What? What's it say?"

"Wait. Let me be sure." He walked from the computer desk in the living room to the paper-strewn end of the dining room table.

"We really have to clean this table one day." He shuffled a few papers, found what he wanted, and returned to the computer. His eyes went back and forth from what was in his hand to the computer screen. He reached over and turned on the printer.

When the start-up humming of the printer died out, Kristy asked, "What are you printing? Tell me. Did she call Pete's cell or not?"

Mark took the one page from the printer. He smiled Kristy's way.

"Moriarty says our two friends are not being interviewed until one in the afternoon. How would you like to take a drive to Pleasantville tomorrow morning, early?"

"I'm not driving anywhere until you stop being so cocky and tell me what you think you found. Did she call Pete's cell or not?"

"I'll have to call Moriarty and let him know, too."

"Mark!"

"All right. All right. She did not. Come to the sofa with me, and I'll show you what Verizon has blessedly memorialized for us."

~ * ~

Early the next afternoon, Mark and Kristy stood in the hallway outside the two small cubicles the Pleasantville police used as interrogation rooms. With them was Lieutenant O'Malley, a uniformed officer named Braddock, and a third man, a stranger, newly arrived. Through the one-way glass they saw Bob at a small table, an untouched cardboard cup of coffee within reach. A uniformed officer stood inside, arms crossed, next to the door. Erin sat in the second interrogation room. A female uniformed officer watched over her.

"Keep your eye on me, and I'll gesture when I want you to come in," said Lieutenant O'Malley. "And make sure you don't stand in front of the video camera. We tape everything. Come in and sit down. I'll save you a chair."

"I'll be ready," Mark assured him.

"This is Mr. Denninger, by the way. He's on loan to us this morning from the state D.A.'s office to help with the questioning. I've told him what you have."

"Nice work, Mr. Louis," Denninger said with a nod.

"Want to look at them?" Mark indicated a folder.

Denninger shook his head. "No need. I'll see them when you come into the room. Let—Bob's his name, right?—Bob and me be surprised together."

"As you wish."

"Ready?" the lieutenant asked.

"Let's go," Denninger replied.

As Mark and Kristy observed the scene through the window, the two men entered the room and sat across from Bob.

"How long do you think it will take?" Kristy asked softly.

"Not long. They need to soften him up, and I don't think he's very hard to begin with."

"Suppose Bob doesn't cave in."

"I don't even want to think about it. If we all do our stuff right, though, he will. He'll have to. There's no way around it for him. Erin won't be able to explain it either. Don't worry. We have them."

Kristy made no reply, and they both directed their attention to the dumb show through the glass.

Lieutenant O'Malley was clearly the more aggressive questioner, Denninger the pacifier.

"Bob doesn't look very comfortable," Kristy commented after a quiet fifteen minutes of observation.

"Maybe they won't even need my help," said Mark.

Bob began shaking his head intensely, and Mark could see his lips pronouncing, "No, no."

The lieutenant stood and gestured toward the one-way glass.

"Oh! They do need me. Here I go," said Mark. "Wish me luck."

"Break a leg." Kristy ran her hand down Mark's arm. She stared through the window and saw the profound shock register on Bob's face when Mark entered the room. She watched the lieutenant make the unnecessary introduction between the two men. Mark began to speak, and Bob's worried eyes stayed on him. After a few minutes, Mark waved an admonitory finger toward Bob and waited for a reply. Bob moved his head slightly and said, "No."

Mark opened the folder he carried and placed a business card in front of Bob. Bob nodded and spoke a few words. Mark placed a larger paper in front of him and put his finger on the paper to direct Bob's attention.

Kristy's forehead bumped against the glass as she tried to get a good look at things. Bob's mouth quivered. The lieutenant spoke, followed by Denninger. For emphasis, the lieutenant slapped the tips of his second and third fingers repeatedly on the paper in front of Bob. Suddenly, Bob covered his face with his hands and began to sob. Kristy took a deep breath and stepped back from the glass.

A few moments later, Mark, the lieutenant, and Denninger passed by Kristy on their way to the interrogation room where Erin waited. In passing, Mark said, "Foul deeds will rise...I'm looking forward to this."

Kristy watched Mark disappear into the second interrogation room along with the other men, and she moved in front of the one-way glass to watch.

When Erin saw Mark, her eyes narrowed, and her face reddened with hatred.

"We have some questions for you, Ms. Blakely," Lieutenant O'Malley began.

"What's he doing here?" she asked, indicating Mark.

"Mr. Louis will also have some questions for you. This is Mr. Denninger from the state D.A's office. He's assisting us on this case. You've rejected having your lawyer present. Is that correct?"

"I don't need a lawyer," Erin said proudly, and O'Malley started in.

"Ms. Blakely, were you involved in the murder of your husband?"

"No."

"Did you involve a Mr. Bob Collins in the murder of your husband?"

"No."

"Did you know Mr. Bob Collins during the time you lived in Pleasantville?"

"No."

After a short pause, the lieutenant said, "Are you certain you want to stick with those answers?"

"Yes."

"Erin," said Mark as the lieutenant and Denninger sat back to watch. "I feel sorry for you and sorrier still for Raven. But this must be."

Erin glared stonily at Mark.

"You were planning to leave your husband, take Raven, and move to New York with Bob long before you ever staged meeting him in front of us at the gallery."

A hint of smugness crept over Erin's features.

"Your invitation to us was part of your scheme. You wanted to get into acting when you moved to New York, so you looked up Kristy when you did. You figured you could ingratiate your way into our company, but Jeremy showed up and set off everything that happened afterward. You were on the cusp of a new life, and having your old life come and slap you in the face must have made you furious. You were afraid Jeremy had some rights to your daughter. You'd be in New York. Who knows where Jeremy would be? If he had a right to see her, you might lose Raven for periods of time to a man you detested, and so you took certain steps, and made quite a bit of money doing so, by the way, much more than you would have gotten if you'd simply left your husband.

"You faked the meeting at the gallery because what both you and Bob did in Pleasantville could have no possible motive if you hadn't known each other there. You managed to get Jeremy and Pete in the same place at the same time by giving your husband the name of the wrong restaurant and by promising to meet Jeremy there. You made certain your cell phone didn't work—you demonstrated that amply for Kristy and me—so your husband couldn't get in touch with you.

"When you first showed us your phone wasn't working, you refused Kristy's offer of her cell phone and said you'd call your husband from home and tell him when and where to meet because, of course, you couldn't possibly have made the call in front of us. We'd have heard you misdirect him. Later, when he was late for dinner, Kristy insisted you try to track him down. You started for the restaurant phone, but Kristy insisted you use her cell phone. You called your house and the car dealership because you knew Pete wouldn't be at either place since you'd told him to be at the other restaurant by, what? Say, six o'clock? You moved away from the table to make a third call. When you came back to the table, you claimed you'd called Pete's cell as well as the home and work numbers. You said he didn't answer his cell. Isn't that right?"

"Exactly so. I couldn't find him." Erin's smugness ate at Mark.

"Going over and over this, your cell phone troubles finally put me on the right track. Since you never really wanted to talk to Pete at all, I knew you couldn't call his cell when you were with us. Just to make certain, I checked.

"Luckily—or in your case, unluckily—Verizon keeps a record of all calls in the customer's account online. I checked and found the four calls you made on Kristy's phone: the first two, looking for Pete at home and work around seven, and the fourth call around eight-thirty to your house again when you received the bad news about Pete. The third call, though, is the problem."

Just as he'd done for Bob, Mark placed Bob's Pleasantville business card and Kristy's phone bill in front of Erin, pointed to the specific call, and felt the beginnings of triumph when Erin's smugness vanished. Her mouth tightened, and she moved uncomfortably in her chair.

"Kristy and I took a trip to Pleasantville one Saturday to check up on Bob. We found he worked in Pleasantville, not Galloway, in the building you went into the first day we picked up Raven from school— the building we saw Bob go into that day after he looked into your car while Kristy and I waited for you. I recognized Bob at the opening but couldn't remember where I'd seen him. Now, it's obvious to me. That same building is the one where Kristy and I saw you say good-bye to a man before you met us for lunch on Main Street. We couldn't see who you were saying good-bye to, but it was clearly a man.

"When Kristy and I checked up on Bob, we found his old office. He'd closed it up by then, but a few of his business cards were still in the little plastic holder outside of the door. You see one of them in front of you. I used the phone number on it to track down the location of Bob's current studio in Brooklyn. I visited him, as he no doubt told you.

So, his Pleasantville studio phone number was fresh in my memory, since I'd just called it. And there it was again, staring me in the face on Kristy's phone bill. I recognized it. Maybe you called to tell him the plan was working. Maybe you called to see whether he'd finished his job and made you a free woman. It doesn't matter why you called. It doesn't even matter if he was there to pick up. You wouldn't have his studio number memorized unless you called it frequently. It becomes obvious, doesn't it, that you knew Bob very well back in Pleasantville—well enough to know his studio number by heart and well enough for him to recognize your car."

Lieutenant O'Malley rose slowly from his chair and gestured at the window. Slowly, the door opened, and Bob stood in the doorway, an officer on each side of him, his face streaked with tears and etched with grief. When Erin's eyes met his, he turned away.

The lieutenant closed the door.

"Oh, my God," Erin moaned, no longer smug or even angry. One word more slipped softly from her lips.

"Raven."

Twenty-two

An hour later, Mark called and informed Jeremy of the day's outcome. Jeremy did not express much surprise over Erin's involvement in the murder of her husband until Mark pointed out that Raven was now his responsibility.

He imposed on Mark to take care of Raven until Christmas day—two days off—while he made necessary preparations. In addition, he begged Mark to break the news about her mother to Raven.

"I don't want Raven's first encounter with me to be my telling her that," he argued.

Mark acceded to his requests, the first with more eagerness than the second. Back in New York, he and Kristy picked up Raven from her babysitter after returning their rental car. They took a cab to their apartment, Mark responding to Raven's asking for her mother by saying he would explain when they got home.

Mark decided there was no way to dance around the explanation.

Erin had done a bad thing and was going to be punished for it in a way that would prevent contact with Raven for a long time.

He repeated the words over and over during the cab ride and repeated them as gently and simply as he could to Raven as he watched the fear and confusion mount in her eyes.

"What bad thing? What did she do?"

"I think you'll have to be a little older to really understand. She hurt somebody, Raven, and no one is allowed to hurt someone the way she did."

Then the tears began. Mark could feel the utter fright and desperation of the child. They were seated on the sofa, and he put his arm around her. She buried her head on his chest and sobbed. Kristy stood in the kitchen doorway and peeked out. She moved toward the living room, but Mark motioned her to stay away.

"But what bad thing did she do? What bad thing did she do? What bad thing did she do?"

The question came like the throbbing agony of a rotten tooth. Mark soothed her as best he could. When Raven was too exhausted to cry any more, she fell asleep in Mark's arms. Mark gently eased himself away from her and let her rest on the sofa.

"The poor kid didn't have a thing to eat," Kristy said softly.

"Me either. Got anything for a sandwich?"

Kristy made sandwiches, and a half-hour later, Mark settled himself into his reading chair, keeping a close eye on Raven.

"Are you coming to bed?" Kristy asked.

"No. She can't wake up in the dark all alone. She didn't like the idea of sleeping out here under the best of circumstances. Leave a little light on."

"You'll manage?"

"I'll manage. Go."

~ * ~

Mark was awake and waiting in his chair when Raven opened her eyes next morning. She stared at him blankly for a moment and quickly bustled up onto his lap.

"You must be hungry. Kristy is making us pancakes."

Mark took Raven into the kitchen and put some breakfast in front of her. Then came a long, slow day Mark would remember as the dreariest day of his life. Raven would not leave his side, so Kristy went out, alone, to get a Christmas tree and presents to put under the tree for Raven.

"I have more to tell you, Raven," Mark said when they were alone.

Raven, who had been staring blankly at cartoons on TV, turned to him, and tears filled her eyes.

Mark stroked her hair. "This is good news. Ready?"

Two tears rolled down Raven's cheeks. Mark took a tissue and wiped them away.

"Your daddy will be here tomorrow, and he'll be taking care of you from now on."

More confusion swept over Raven's face. "My daddy?"

"You have one, you know."

"Mommy...Mommy said he went away and wouldn't be back."

Mark felt a spasm of anger toward Erin. "Well, he's come back. He's come back especially to take care of you, and he'll be here tomorrow. You've seen him once before, only you didn't know he was your daddy then. Do you remember the man who came to your house before we ate dinner when Kristy and I visited? Remember him?"

"When Mommy dropped her glass of wine?"

"Yes."

Raven gave a slight shrug.

"I'm pretty sure you'll be the only little girl in New York City who's getting a daddy for Christmas."

Raven digested the news and turned back to the TV.

Mark stared at her and wondered how she could possibly process all the information he'd poured into her in these last eighteen hours. All in all, though, she seemed to be holding up reasonably well. Thank heaven, because if Raven started crying again today like she'd cried yesterday, Mark thought he might take a flying leap from the nearest open window.

At night, they trimmed the tree, and after Raven fell asleep in the big bed, Mark and Kristy wrapped the presents Kristy had bought for her and placed them under the tree. The next morning, Raven opened her presents with a limited degree of enthusiasm. When she finished opening her final present, she asked, "Where's my daddy?"

"Did you expect to find him wrapped in paper under the tree with your other presents?" Mark asked with a smile.

Raven shook her head but did not smile.

"He'll be here at noon, in an hour."

A few minutes before noon, the apartment buzzer sounded. Raven stopped playing, ran to Mark, and climbed next to him on the sofa. He put his arm around her, and together they stared at the apartment door. Kristy moved greet the guest.

"Get ready," Mark whispered.

The door opened, and Jeremy stood in the doorway looking like a tableau of Christmas giving. He carried a stuffed panda under one arm and a shopping bag full of gifts in the other. He and Raven stared at one another, still as statues. Finally, he stepped over the threshold, put the shopping bag down, and presented the panda to Raven.

"I hope you like it. I'm your father. I'm sorry, so sorry I've been away so long. I promise not to go away again."

Raven took the bear and put it in her lap. She stayed at Mark's side.

"These presents are for you. Santa left them with me because he knew I'd be seeing you today."

Raven pointed toward the brightly lit tree. "He left some here, too."

Jeremy smiled. "Oh, wow. You get double!" He took the presents from the bag and spread them out on the coffee table. "Open them whenever you want."

When Raven didn't move, Mark leaned over, took one of the presents and handed it to her. She opened it and, one by one, the others.

Mark patted Raven's head. "Santa's been very good to you."

"I have more good news," Jeremy said. "But not from Santa."

Mark could hear the tension in his voice.

"You and I are going to live in your apartment. The one where you live now. Your mom said we could. She didn't want you to have to change your school or move anywhere. She said you like where you live now. I hope you do."

Raven gave a curt nod.

A pang of sympathy shot through Mark. Another two tons of information for her to deal with.

While Raven was occupied with her gifts, Jeremy took Mark and Kristy aside.

"They let Erin call me yesterday—about the apartment."

"She say anything else?" Mark asked.

"She asked me to take good care of Raven."

Kristy made lunch, and everyone ate at the table. Midway through the meal, Raven asked Mark, "Will you still babysit me?"

"You bet I will. You'll still be living real nearby."

Jeremy cut in. "Maybe Mark will let you stay here another day or two while I get everything ready at home. I have to move my stuff there and do some other things." He looked at Mark.

Mark smiled. "Of course. Okay with you?" he asked Raven, who answered with the first hint of a smile since she'd arrived in the apartment the day before. "Take as long as you need, Jeremy."

"I'll stop by every day, Raven, and in a few days, we'll go back home."

Raven gave another tiny nod. Jeremy stayed through dinner, and afterward, gave Raven an awkward kiss and left.

Raven yawned, and Kristy got her ready for bed. Mark took her into the bedroom and tucked her in.

"Everything will be all right, Raven, you'll see. Your daddy seems like a very nice fellow." He considered mentioning the two probably very generous grandparents who were part of her Christmas package, but decided to leave that detail for Jeremy.

Raven yawned again. "You're a nice fellow, too." She put her hand in his.

Mark gave her tiny hand a squeeze. "Thank you. Want to hear about those careless kittens again?"

Raven agreed, but halfway through the first reading, she fell asleep.

Kristy lay on the sofa, her eyes closed.

Mark squeezed in next to her. "Hey, you're a real ball of energy, sweetie. If you lost your mittens, you'd never find them."

"What are you going to do about the play?" Kristy asked.

"I already called Karen, and she's ready to take over Erin's part, and she has a friend Rachel, remember her?"

"I do."

"She'll take over Karen's part. We'll rehearse her hard next week. We'll be all right, and what a pleasure it'll be to get back to some semblance of normal."

"Not the most cheerful Christmas Day we'll ever have, is it?" she whispered.

"A sad tale's best for winter, as our play points out. Quite a surprise about the apartment, eh?"

"I suppose Erin loves Raven more than she hates Jeremy, but let's not talk about it. Snuggle next to me." Mark obeyed and snuggled closer to Kristy, who kissed him and whispered, "If we're real quiet, I think it's time for me to give you the Christmas present I've saved till last."

"You don't mean right here and now, do you?"

"I do. Can't give it to you in the bedroom, can I? It's occupied."

"True."

"Dining table might give us splinters, right?"

"Sadly true."

"Then, shhhhhh. Unwrap your gift slowly and enjoy it quietly." She pressed her lips against Mark's, and for the next hour or so, Mark enjoyed, as he later told Kristy, the best Christmas gift Santa had ever given him.

Meet John Paulits

John Paulits lives in New York City and spent many years there teaching. He has written fiction for over forty years, novels for children as well as adults. *A Spider Steeped* is his fifteenth book for WingsePress. To learn more about John's books, visit him at: www.johnpaulits.com.

Other Works From The Pen Of

John Paulits

For ages 8-12

Philip Gets Even - By accident at an art show in which they are entered, Philip Felton and Emery Wyatt offend Johnny Visco, the toughest boy in sixth grade, and he promises to get even. When Johnny Visco's attacks show no sign of stopping, Philip, Emery, and Mr. Conway concoct a plan that finally puts Johnny Visco in his place and prevents him from tormenting the boys any longer.

Philip and the Case of Mistaken Identity - Philip and his best friend Emery, detectives on the trail, try to cope with a mystifying little girl who runs them a merry chase.

The Director - The Director invites nine-year-old Tommy Whitaker to be a character in a book set in 1957. The trouble begins in the Regal movie theatre, where after the Saturday matinee. Elwood Wambo, the strange caretaker of the movie theatre, hires Tommy and his 1957 best friend, Mouse, to stay behind on future Saturdays to clean the theatre when the movie is over. The boys later learn that Wambo and his partner Jeremy are part of a gang of thieves. When their friend Smitty's bike is stolen and when Smitty himself mysteriously disappears, Tommy and his two friends, Mouse and Royal, vow to solve the mysteries of their missing friend, his missing bike...and a murder.

A Cat Tale - Hayden and his fellow cats find their way to paradise: Talula Tupperman's Home for Distressed Felines. But Rodney and Stanley, cat kidnappers, are on their trail, and suddenly cats begin to vanish. Can Hayden and his troop put a stop to these mysterious disappearances before they mysteriously vanish, too?

The Mountaintop - Jason, a seventeen-year-old Amerian, sets out for the mountaintop to determine the truth of his people's beliefs. On his journey he runs into some unexpected and eye-opening adventures. Most importantly, he meets Manda, a 17-year-old Ginder girl, who changes his life irrevocably.

For adults

Hobson's Planet - When Culp Robinson arrives on the Hobson's Planet, he steps into a whirlwind of controversy and political upheaval. Against his will, Culp finds himself the designated savior to another planet. Having failed on Earth, he wants no part of another such quest. Now he must decide where his duty and his heart lie.

Henny and Lloyd Private Eyes - Henny and Lloyd, age mid-twenties, have completed their online course in private detecting and are now licensed PIs. They've rented an office on Centre Street in downtown NYC, a rundown apartment each in Williamsburg, Brooklyn, and now set out to make their dreams of crime-fighting come true.

Ant-Nee's Golden Notebook - Mayhem and mix-ups follow Bruno Brunotaglia's murder of a hit man sent after him by a rival mob. Panic stricken, Bruno leaves behind a briefcase of money and an import notebook. Two down-and-out friends find the briefcase and notebook, and Bruno needs them back before his father, head of the Philly mob, blows a gasket. Will Richard get to keep the briefcase of money he found with Strangler and the Indian hard on his trail? Can Clarence make hay from the information in the notebook? It's a battle of half-wits in this deadly game of hide and seek.

The Sad Case of Brownie Terwilliger - Brownie Terwilliger looks at his opportunity of running for mayor of Philadelphia as a chance to right the wrongs of a city. He hopes to oust Milton Streezo, the incumbent, but Streezo does not take kindly to this challenge and concocts a plan to destroy Brownie, even hiring Lunky Ledbetter, famed perpetrator of dirty political tricks. Can Brownie withstand the onslaught? Will he have the opportunity to do some good in the world? Don't bet on it.

The Collected Short Stories - A man buried alive; the extinction of a gloried species; the mingling of interstellar races; a mysterious amulet; a fearful child; an animal-loving old hag; the assassination of the Almighty. Stories of horror, mystery, fantasy, and science fiction certain to raise the hairs on your neck.

The Rest is Silence – The Shakespeare Murders, Vol 1
When a body is found on the stage of the Bouwerie Lane Theatre, the AWB Theatre is thrown into turmoil, and Don Lovett, one of its actors, is suspected of murder. Can AWB actor Mark Louis exonerate his good friend and bring the life of the acting troupe back to normal?

A Dying Fall – The Shakespeare Murders, Vol. 2 When the AWB Theatre troupe accepts an invitation to perform on the tropical island of Illyria, they get more than they bargained for. Sudden death. The actors, however, must return home to New York, forcing company member Mark Louis to conduct his investigation a thousand miles from the crime.

To Prove a Villain – The Shakespeare Murders, Vol. 3
When Mark Louis investigates the death of Kristy King's brother, what he learns upends their theatre company as well as his relationship with Kristy. Should he have let sleeping dogs lie?

Letter to Our Readers

Enjoy this book?

You can make a difference.

As an independent publisher, Wings ePress, Inc. does not have the financial clout of the large New York publishers. We can't afford large magazine spreads or subway posters to tell people about our quality books.

But we do have something much more effective and powerful than ads. We have a large base of loyal readers.

Honest reviews help bring the attention of new readers to our books.

If you enjoyed this book, we would appreciate it if you would spend a few minutes posting a review on the site where you purchased this book or on the Wings ePress, Inc. webpages at:
https://wingsepress.com/

Thank You

Visit Our Website

For The Full Inventory
Of Quality Books:

Wings ePress, Inc

Quality trade paperbacks and downloads
in multiple formats, in genres ranging from
light romantic comedy to general fiction and horror.
Wings has something for every reader's taste.
Visit the website, then bookmark it.
We add new titles each month!

Wings ePress Inc.
3000 N. Rock Road
Newton, KS 67114